I0521480

Enforcer Rigel Patterson is known around Shifter Headquarters as a playboy, and he's okay with that. After all, he doesn't think there's anything wrong with enjoying himself while he waits for Fate to deliver his mate to him. While at a club, Rigel is thrilled when She finally delivers the other half of his soul to him—a handsome human named Tucker. Rigel quickly whisks his mate out of the club, enjoying a night of passion. Except, upon waking the next morning, he finds Tucker gone. Rigel realizes that he should have done a little more talking, but it's too late.

He enlists the aid of friends to help him find Tucker. When Rigel runs across Tucker by accident, he's overjoyed. In his enthusiasm, he accidentally outs Tucker to his parents. After an explosive display, Rigel realizes explaining he's an alligator shifter, mates, and the paranormal world could be the least of his problems. Can Rigel convince Tucker to forgive him and give them a chance?

The unauthorized reproduction or distribution of this copyrighted work is illegal. Criminal copyright infringement, including infringement without monetary gain, is investigated by the FBI and is punishable by up to 5 years in federal prison and a fine of $250,000.

This book is a work of fiction. Names, characters, places, and incidents either are products of the author's imagination or are used fictitiously. Any resemblance to actual events or locales or persons, living or dead, is entirely coincidental.

An Amant for the Alligator
Copyright © 2023 Charlie Richards
ISBN: 978-1-4874-4087-9
Cover art by Angela Waters

All rights reserved. Except for use in any review, the reproduction or utilization of this work in whole or in part in any form by any electronic, mechanical or other means, now known or hereafter invented, is forbidden without the written permission of the publisher.

Published by eXtasy Books Inc

Look for us online at:
www.eXtasybooks.com

An Amant for the Alligator Shifter's Regime: Book Fourteen

By

Charlie Richards

DEDICATION

*Progress is impossible without change, and those who cannot
change their minds cannot change anything.*
~George Bernard Shaw

CHAPTER ONE

"Hey, handsome."

Rigel Patterson snapped his attention from Lydia's firm-looking butt and met her gaze. The brunette's smile appeared flirty and welcoming. Unable to help himself, Rigel grinned broadly at her. After all, he'd been caught staring at her ass . . . ets, and he'd never been shy about the fact that he enjoyed sex.

Before Rigel could bother answering, Lydia turned and headed out the hallway door and into the outdoors. He figured she was heading to work. Lydia had recently been hired on at Shifter Council Headquarters as a member of the grounds team—the council hid their operations with the appearance of the place being a high-end, exclusive golf resort and day spa.

As Lydia slipped out the door, Rigel allowed his gaze to once again fall to her backside. She really did have a nice ass. Watching her disappear, Rigel was certain she swayed her hips just a little extra.

Chuckling, Rigel shook his head. As pretty as the slender, toned Lydia was, she didn't really do it for him. He just happened to appreciate looking at a nice body. Lydia was a brunette, and so was Rigel. Call him picky, but Rigel preferred blonds—men or women didn't matter. He liked seeing the contrast in their colorings as their naked bodies moved against each other.

Just thinking of the last blonde Rigel had enjoyed—a petite, slightly plump woman with gorgeous tits—he felt his prick

1

begin plumping in his jeans.

"Uh, word of advice."

Link's deep voice cut into Rigel's thoughts, and he turned his attention to his friend. The large musk ox shifter worked in the cyber division of shifter headquarters, and the large shifter eyed Rigel with a look of concern. Link even rubbed his palm over his bald scalp as he furrowed his brows.

"Sure, man," Rigel replied, patting him on the arm, hoping to calm him. "What's the advice?"

"Don't get seduced by Lydia," Link muttered after a quick glance around. He dipped his head, closing the inch height difference between them, and whispered into his ear, "Heard some things about her. Uh, she's looking for a mate."

Rigel eyed Link thoughtfully, trying to connect the dots as Link gave him a meaningful look. "Aren't we all looking for our Fated mate?" he asked slowly. "I know I am."

While Rigel knew a number of those working on and for the shifter council considered him a player, he still wanted his mate. He just figured he would enjoy what others offered before he found that special someone. Once the other half of his soul came along, that would be it, and Rigel would never stray.

I can't wait, no matter what others think of me.

"No, not Fated mate," Link countered with a shake of his heavily bearded head. His deep brown eyes held a troubled gleam. "I mean, she wants a mate. A child. A family. A guy to give her that and support her." After another glance around, Link touched Rigel's lower back and began guiding him out of the dining hall where they'd just finished their lunch. "I mean."

Another glance to the left caused Link to snap his mouth shut. Discreetly looking that way, Rigel spotted Councilman Georgio Peregrine. The elk shifter had shared the belief that Fate didn't pair those of the same sex until it was proven otherwise. Still, Rigel knew that behind closed doors, Georgio continued to spout anti-homosexual remarks.

Few council enforcers enjoyed their time guarding the man, but a job was a job. When it was Rigel's rotation to accompany Georgio while the man was on headquarters' grounds, he did it to the best of his ability. Rigel also paid careful attention to who Georgio met with, hoping he could compile some information to get the bigoted councilman booted from his seat.

Rigel knew most of the other enforcers were doing the same. So far, nothing the elk shifter did while he'd been watching him had been questionable. It made Rigel wonder if he saved any unsavory meetings for when he was guarded by one of his three favorites.

Through whispers from friends, Rigel had learned that Investigator Paul Stiggard was transferring to the enforcer ranks. He claimed he wanted to stay closer to home and friends. As Paul was a favorite of Georgio's, it would make sense that the councilman would ask for the bear shifter's services often.

What Georgio didn't know, and Rigel had only found out by accident, was that Paul was as gay as the day was long.

While Rigel didn't know why Paul continued to hide his sexuality after several councilmen ended up with male Fated mates — enforcers, too — Rigel supposed Paul's continued subterfuge would help them.

Once the cafeteria doors were closed behind them and they were striding down the hall, Link picked up where he'd left off. "I hear Lydia plans to get an enforcer to knock her up, then insist on being taken care of."

Rigel gaped for a second before snapping his mouth shut. Snorting, he shook his head. "No way that would work on most of us." He smirked at his friend. "Enforcers are known to be very careful. Can't tell you how grateful I was for the invention of the condom."

Link chuckled low in his throat, the deep sound rumbling from him. "Me, too." Just as quickly, he sobered as he warned, "But I hear she's putting holes in the ones she carries so they fail."

"Oh, for fuck's sake," Rigel growled, glaring over his shoulder in the general direction of where Lydia had probably gone. "And she's still working here?"

"No proof," Link told him with a shrug. "Would just be a he-said, she-said situation."

Rigel gritted his teeth as he scowled at the floor. He knew Link was right, but it still sucked. The woman could prove to be a danger to one of his friends who enjoyed brunettes and ended up snared by her wiles.

"I'll pass it on," Rigel murmured, thinking of which of his buddies were the most likely candidates. "Thanks for telling me, Link." As the musk ox shifter nodded once, Rigel scoffed softly. "Of course, I wasn't in any danger from her. I'm partial to blonds, remember?"

"I know." Link smirked at him, his brown eyes gleaming with mirth. "Doesn't mean you wouldn't accept some quick action if it'd been a while for you."

Even as Rigel opened his mouth to deny that, an altercation with a black-haired human with an ass to die for popped into his head. He grinned at Link instead and offered an unrepentant shrug. His buddy knew him well.

Link chuckled.

Pausing at a T-junction, Rigel patted Link's upper arm with the back of his hand. "You coming to *The Amnesty* tonight?"

Rigel referred to a shifter-owned-and-operated night club. It catered to both the gay and straight crowd, with the occasional specialty night for fringe groups. Rigel and a number of others frequented it at least twice a month.

When Rigel noticed Link hesitating, he nudged him with his elbow. "Come on, man. Come hang with us." With a smirk, he told him, "I'm sure I can help you find a cute twink to suck that mammoth cock you're hiding." Rigel glanced meaningfully at his big friend's crotch, knowing exactly what the guy was packing.

While Rigel had never slept with Link, he'd seen him while shifting more times than he could count. Considering the size of the man's big piece of meat while flaccid, he could only guess at his length and girth while erect. In truth, Rigel had no desire to ever find out.

Rigel wasn't a bottom, as a rule, and the idea of fitting a pole the size that he suspected Link sported when in need made his ass clench uncomfortably. Still, he knew there were plenty of men who considered themselves size queens. While Rigel knew there were women out there who thought taking a man Link's size would be a challenge to accept, he knew his buddy preferred men.

Seeing Link's medium-tanned cheeks and neck darken a bit, coupled with the scent of embarrassment in the air, Rigel rolled his eyes. "Come on, man." He offered his buddy a cajoling grin. "It's been too long since ya joined us. It'll be me, Lyra, Dakota, and Charon"—Rigel paused to wink—"Delanrue and Miggs are on baby-sitting duty tonight. Plus, there'll be a few others from our crowd." With a grin, Rigel punched Link's upper arm again. In truth, he wasn't entirely certain who all would be there, but it'd been nearly three weeks since he'd jammed on the dance floor, and he couldn't wait. "It'll be fun."

After heaving a breath, Link nodded once. "Okay." He shoved his big hands into the pockets of his jeans. "What time?"

Grinning broadly, Rigel took a step backward toward the south hallway. "Seven o'clock at Jin's place," he told him, referring to fellow enforcer Tideus's mate Sinjin's restaurant—*The Dancing Leprechaun*. "He has the back room reserved for us."

Rigel thought Tideus's mate had a gift. Sinjin—Jin to his friends—owned, operated, and worked as the chef for an authentic Irish-themed restaurant and pub. Rigel couldn't think of a place with better food.

Hmmm . . . perfect date place . . . if I ever find my mate.

Hearing Link rumble, "I'll see you there," pulled Rigel from his random thought.

Geez. Why do I keep thinking about finding my mate so much lately? Must be because so many other guys have found theirs. Makes me feel wishful.

Giving his mind a mental shake, Rigel gave Link two thumbs up before turning and heading down the hallway.

After several shots of *Patron* and a half dozen beers, Rigel felt a mild buzz and was grateful he'd caught a ride with fellow enforcer, Lyra. He knew it wouldn't last long, considering his shifter metabolism. Still, it felt nice to know his buddies would keep an eye on him while he cut loose for a few hours.

"Ready to head to the club?" Lyra asked, a grin curving her tanned features as she rose to her feet. She wriggled her hips as she danced in place. "I'm ready to get my groove on."

Rigel pulled his attention away from a pretty blond man sitting at a table with a few others. "Yup." Rising, he glanced around, seeing he was the last to stand.

"Already distracted by eye candy, Rigel?" Enforcer Dakota teased, waggling his brows as he glanced pointedly at the man Rigel had been watching. "Probably not the place for a pick-up."

Curving his lips into a wide grin, Rigel replied unabashedly, "Just enjoyin' the view." He barely resisted cupping his half-hard prick as he teased, "Plannin' to get laid tonight, so I'm warmin' up."

Lyra rolled her eyes as Dakota barked a laugh. Charon

smirked as he shook his head. Dakota's middle brother, Dane, snorted as he slung his arm over the shoulders of his blushing mate, Danny. The young human looked at the floor, unable to meet Rigel's eyes.

Rigel patted Danny on the shoulder lightly. "Sorry, Danny," he offered, lowering his voice. "I forget you're not used to our crude humor quite yet."

Before meeting and bonding with Dane, Danny had been a shy virgin. While he was no longer a virgin, he was still shy. Dane was slowly helping his human come out of his shell, introducing him to the world, since Danny had grown up in a small, repressive backwater town.

"It's fine, Rigel," Danny murmured, a small smile teasing the corners of his lips as he met Rigel's eyes for an instant before lowering his gaze again. "No need to change for me."

"You're so sweet, my mate," Dane rumbled. He dipped his head and pressed a kiss to Danny's temple. "Never change, love."

The look Danny bestowed upon Dane could only be called radiant.

Rigel looked away, feeling a pang of jealousy curl through his gut. As much as he liked exploring the body of a new lover, he wanted what some of his friends had found. He wanted his one and only.

Knowing he had to be patient and wait for Fate's timing, Rigel shoved the feeling way down deep.

"Come on, Casanova," Lyra teased, slinging her arm around Rigel's waist. "Let's go to the club so we can both find hotties."

"Sounds good to me," Rigel stated agreeably, happy for the distraction. He wrapped his arm around Lyra's waist in return. As they started out of Jin's restaurant, Rigel asked, "Who do I owe for dinner?"

"Dakota picked up the tab, telling us it's their treat because it's their date night," Lyra told him while wrinkling her nose, betraying how she felt about that. "So we're gonna buy all their drinks at the bar."

Rigel winced. If he'd known he wasn't paying his own way, he wouldn't have drank quite so much. "I'll have to slip one of 'em a hundred when they're not lookin'," he muttered, shaking his head.

"Yeah." Lyra snickered. "Good luck with that."

Vowing to find his moment, Rigel opened the door for Lyra and followed her out of the restaurant.

Twenty minutes later, Rigel held the door for her again as they entered the club. The music thrummed in his ear drums, making him fight back a wince. Sometimes, there were downsides to being a shifter and having superior hearing.

On the other hand, when Rigel drew a deep breath into his lungs, he appreciated his shifter sense of smell. His senses were instantly flooded by a mixture of alcohol, male sweat, and arousal. Rigel inhaled again, enjoying the heady mixture.

His body reacted faster than he could ever remember, his blood instantly flooding his dick. He reached down and adjusted himself as his cock swelled to full mast in seconds.

When Lyra arched a brow and smirked at him, Rigel had to fight to keep himself from doing something he hadn't done in decades—blush.

With a shrug, Rigel admitted, "There's something in the air."

"In the air?" Lyra cocked her head as she gave him a questioning look. "Other than the usual pheromones?"

"Uh . . . "

Was there?

"No," Rigel began before inhaling again. "It's just—"

His mouth began to water, and his alligator rumbled in his mind.

"You sure?" Lyra eyed him curiously as she guided Rigel deeper into the club.

Rigel hadn't even realized he'd stopped just inside the foyer.

"Everything okay?" Dane asked, dropping into step on Rigel's other side. The big Komodo dragon shifter swept his gaze over Rigel's face and seemed concerned about the expression there. "Should we get you a glass of water?"

Rigel gaped at Dane for an instant before snapping his mouth shut. "Water?" he repeated inanely.

Rigel shook his head hard, as if that would help him clear it. His brain finally started clicking again, and the realization hit him like a two-by-four upside the head. Staring at Dane, Rigel uttered words he'd been waiting decades to say.

"I think I scent my mate."

CHAPTER TWO

"**I**'m gonna go dance." Tucker Rolden leaned across the table and had to nearly shout the words to his sister — Amelia — so she could hear him over the pounding of the club's music. "Wanna join me?"

"No thanks, birthday boy," Amelia called back with a smile. She tapped her daiquiri glass with one mauve-painted fingernail. "I wanna finish my drink first."

After a nod, Tucker rose to his feet. He'd downed his own fruity drink fairly quickly. He didn't get to enjoy them often, as his dad was a beer drinker and thought any other beverage wasn't manly. Tucker could only imagine what his father would say about his desire to find a guy to fuck him for the night.

And hopefully, dear ol' dad'll never learn I'm bi.

Pushing thoughts of his bigoted father from his mind, Tucker headed toward the dance floor. He planned to enjoy the evening of his twenty-sixth birthday. To do that, Tucker intended to dance for a while and find a hot body to rub against.

And if all goes well, I'll get to enjoy more than that later.

With that thought firmly in mind, Tucker slipped onto the dance floor. He quickly lost himself in the sea of writhing bodies. Lifting his arms, Tucker tipped his head back and gyrated his hips in time to the pounding music.

It wasn't long before Tucker felt hands land on his waist and a body slip up behind him. A glance over his shoulder revealed a tall, slender black male. Tucker met the man's dark-eyed gaze and smiled.

Tucker turned his back on the man again and pushed his ass into his groin. Falling into sync with his dance partner, they ground together in time to the music. The guy wrapped his arms around Tucker and began feeling up his stomach, causing Tucker's body to simmer with pleasure.

As they continued into the second song, Tucker realized his prick wasn't getting into it. He didn't know why, but he didn't feel much in the way of chemistry for the man.

Evidently, the stranger felt the same way. After the song ended, the guy pressed a kiss to the side of Tucker's neck. "Thanks for the dance, cutie," he rumbled into Tucker's ear. Then he released Tucker and began dancing toward the edge of the dance floor.

Tucker couldn't say that he minded.

Oh, well. There's plenty of fish in the sea.

Through half-closed eyelids, Tucker checked out the prospects around him as he continued to dance. He noticed a dark-haired man a few feet away dancing alone. The guy was several inches taller than Tucker's own five-foot-eleven, had wide shoulders, and a bit of a paunch.

I wonder if his dick is proportionate to his height?

Before Tucker could decide if he wanted to find out, he felt another set of hands on his hips. He didn't get the chance to look behind him before he felt a pair of lips press against the side of his neck. Whoever was behind him wrapped his arms around his waist and pulled him against a broad, hard body.

"You smell so good, handsome," a deep voice purred into Tucker's ear. Large hands slid under Tucker's shirt, and the big man began brazenly teasing his fingers over the skin of Tucker's stomach. "Feel good, too. Knew you would."

Tucker tipped his head to the side, enjoying the tingling sensations the man's mouth was creating on his neck. "Smell good?" he murmured, arching his head a little so he could look at who held him. Tucker could hardly believe that. "Been dancing. I'm sweaty."

"Just makes your delicious scent stronger," the man replied, lifting his head to peer at him with intense, deep-brown eyes. He grinned, showing off even white teeth. "Absolutely perfect."

The look of open appreciation on the handsome stranger's face nearly took Tucker's breath away. The guy's dark hair was pulled away from his face in a ponytail, revealing high, aristocratic cheekbones, not to mention the hungry expression etched over the guy's features. The man was handsome as hell. Considering the hard body pressed against Tucker's backside and the thickly muscled limbs holding him, he would bet the man was ripped.

Bet he knows it, too.

A man as confident and forward as this guy was probably expected to get whatever he wanted.

And it looks like, tonight, he wants me. Huh.

With the erotic tingles dancing across his stomach and causing his cock to harden and twitch in his jeans, Tucker was okay with that. He was there for a pick-up, after all. Considering the guy's hotness factor, Tucker felt a little flattered.

Hmmm . . . happy birthday to me.

Turning in the man's arms, Tucker enjoyed the way the guy kept his hands under his shirt. He massaged over Tucker's lower back and the knobs of his spine. Tucker wrapped his arms around the big stranger's neck and used the hold to urge the man to dip his head again.

To Tucker's surprised pleasure, the guy went with it easily. He expected the man to turn his head and tilt his ear next to Tucker's mouth. Tucker opened his mouth, ready to say something witty or provocative.

Instead, the guy sealed his lips over Tucker's own.

For an instant, Tucker froze. He'd never kissed a guy before. They'd all been one-night stands, and none of them had seemed interested in more than getting their rocks off.

The guy slid his tongue between Tucker's slightly parted lips. He teased it along Tucker's own, causing the hairs on Tucker's nape to stand on end. Finally, when the man nipped at Tucker's lower lip, causing a tremble to work through him, Tucker snapped out of his surprise.

Tilting his chin a little, Tucker began kissing the man back. He tightened his hold on the guy's neck, clutching at him. Pressing into the kiss, he began doing a little exploring of his own.

Tucker couldn't help but groan as he registered the man's taste. He recognized hints of tequila mixed with something deeper, something masculine that had to be all the guy's own. The robust flavor lit up Tucker's taste buds, and he wanted more of it.

Feeling the guy grip his ass and lift, flushing their bodies tightly together, Tucker grunted with pleasure. The hard ridge pressing against his own sent a zing up his spine. His dick ached behind the fly of his jeans, and he instinctively rocked his hips, searching for friction.

"Rigel." The deep voice caused Tucker's prospective hook-up to snap his head up, ending the kiss. The man didn't release him even as he looked left at an even larger man with shaggy blond hair. While the guy was looking at his prospective hook-up with amusement dancing in his brown eyes, he cautioned, "Mauling him on the dance floor may not be the best decision."

The guy holding Tucker winced as he jerked a nod. He refocused on Tucker and gave him a wry smile. "You make me forget myself," he told him in a gruff voice. "That hasn't happened in a long damn time." After squeezing Tucker's ass cheek once more, the guy relaxed his grip and slid his hand up to palm his lower back. "Come home with me?"

Even though that was exactly what Tucker wanted to do, he still hesitated. He hadn't gone home with a trick since he was a young, dumb college student. The guy had ended up fighting with him about condoms coupled with being a dud in the sack.

A bathroom or back-alley hook-up never questioned the use of condoms.

"Please, my handsome mate," the man urged, his tone turning sensual. "I want to love on you all night long." Dipping his head, he crooned into Tucker's ear, "Find all your hot spots. Make you cry my name as I send you flying with bliss."

God, that sounds amazing.

"Please?"

This man should never have to beg.

Still, Tucker knew he had to protect himself.

"We'll have to agree to a couple of rules," Tucker declared.

"Anything you want," the guy vowed without hesitation.

"I give my sister your address," Tucker told him, eyeing for his reaction. "That way someone knows where I am."

The man immediately nodded. "Of course." While concern filled his eyes, he stated, "It's always good to have someone aware of where you're going . . . with a stranger." Then he curved his lips into a hungry smile. "Although, we won't be strangers for much longer."

Unable to help it, Tucker felt warmth begin to creep up his neck. "Uh, o-okay." Then he cleared his throat and ordered, "And you'll wear a condom." Tucker narrowed his eyes and insisted, "Non-negotiable. I don't do bareback."

As Tucker watched, he spotted the big men exchanging glances. They even seemed to be speaking silently to each other, considering the way his dance partner arched a brow, while the other guy narrowed his eyes and tipped his head, followed by his prospective hook-up dipping his chin. He wondered at just how long the pair had known each other.

Do they know each other . . . like that?

To Tucker's surprise, a surge of jealousy—which he totally wanted to deny—rushed through him.

Damn. Weird.

His possible hook-up for the evening focused on Tucker and nodded. He also rubbed up and down his spine . . . under his shirt again. The guy even offered him a roguish grin.

"Anything to get my hands on you, handsome," he told him.

Tucker's heart pounded, and his prick twitched behind his fly. Still, he had to be certain of one more request.

"And no rough stuff." Tucker thought he'd whispered the words, and he prepared to say his request again. *Damn, so embarrassing.* Except, both men exchanged looks as if they'd heard him. When his dance partner immediately began to nod while looking concerned, Tucker added, "I'm not into pain."

"Of course," the big, dark-haired hottie stated, his brows furrowing. At the same time, he rubbed his fingers through Tucker's hair. "I'd never hurt you, handsome."

The guy's friend scoffed, his expression turning dark. "Hell, you're the safest person in the world with Rigel here." The shaggy blond jerked his chin to indicate Tucker's future hook-up. The larger man's eyes narrowed, and his lips curved into a smile that looked almost feral. "Anyone who tried to hurt you, though?" The man snarled as he let out a dark snicker. "Well, they'd be in for a world of hurt." The guy patted Rigel on a thick shoulder. "My buddy, here, is mighty protective of those he cares about."

But he doesn't know me. Why would that extend to me?

Instead of asking that, Tucker decided to give in to his dick's aching urging. "Well, then. I guess we oughta stop by my table and give your address to my sister."

"Sounds like a perfect plan," Rigel replied. Then he winced and asked, "Did you drive? I caught a ride with a friend." An abashed expression crossed his face for an instant as he admitted, "I wasn't expecting to meet someone I'd want to take home with me."

Tucker wasn't entirely certain he understood the innuendo

in the guy's comment—Rigel, if his friend was to be believed. It was obvious that the handsome man was there for some stress relief, just as Tucker was. He wondered what had made Rigel decide Tucker was someone he wanted to take home.

Unfortunately, Tucker had to reply, "Afraid not. It's my birthday, so my sister drove so I could drink."

Tucker would never drink more than a beer or two before getting behind the wheel. Working at his father's car dealership with an attached garage, he'd seen far too many vehicles come in that had been damaged by drunk or otherwise impaired driving. Some things just weren't worth the risk.

"You wanna borrow my ride, Rigel?" Rigel's friend offered, holding up a set of keys. "Danny and I can catch a lift with one of the others."

Rigel released Tucker's neck where he'd been gently massaging his nape after he'd finished threading his fingers through his hair. Reaching for the keys, he stated, "I really appreciate it, Dane." He grinned and added, "Not a scratch. I promise."

Continuing to hang onto the keys even after Rigel had closed his fingers around them, the guy—Dane—asked, "You sober, Rigel?"

That was when Tucker recalled the taste of tequila on Rigel's tongue. How many had he had? Maybe he shouldn't be driving, either.

His expression turning serious, Rigel claimed, "Dane, I'm as sober as a cow with a prod up his ass."

Dane scoffed and released the keys. "Have a good night, man." Then his smile appeared truly genuine as he glanced between them and offered, "Congrats, Rigel."

"Thanks, Dane," Rigel replied, sounding just as happy and sincere.

Okay. That's weird.

Before Tucker could think up a way to ask about that, Rigel

slid the hand from under his shirt to around his waist. He settled it on Tucker's opposite hip and began guiding them off the dance floor. As they moved, Rigel bussed a kiss to Tucker's temple.

Damn. He's touchy-feely.

Tucker realized he liked it.

"Where's your sister at?" Rigel asked.

Eager for the night to get moving in the direction his dick wanted, Tucker indicated toward the left. He weaved between tables, and Rigel stayed right with him, not releasing him for a second. Fortunately, Tucker found Amelia right where he'd left her, even though her drink was now empty. A man sat beside her, sitting close, his head bent so he could speak into her ear.

Huh. Guess she's interested in a little action, too.

"Hey, Amelia." Tucker interrupted whatever the man was saying. "You okay there?"

Tucker was still the big brother.

Amelia lifted her attention to Tucker, a slight flush to her cheeks. "Hey, Tuck. I'm good." After a glance between them, she grinned. "What about you?" Amelia looked pointedly at Rigel's possessive hold.

"Yeah, good," Tucker claimed, doing his best to fight down his own blush. His sister had known what he'd hoped for when she'd accompanied him to the club, after all. "So, uh, my date and I are going to head out. I wanted to give you his address."

Amelia's brows shot up, but she nodded. "Of course." She knew how the game was played. After pulling out her phone, she tapped it a few times. Then Amelia peered at Rigel expectantly. "Okay. Address?"

Rigel rattled off an address, and Amelia typed it into her phone.

"Okay," Amelia repeated. Focusing on Tucker, she urged, "Stay safe?"

Tucker nodded. "What about you?" He glanced at the auburn-haired man sitting beside her.

"This is Josh," Amelia told him, her light blush returning. "We're just exchanging numbers, is all." She rose. "I'll walk out with you." Turning to Josh, Amelia smiled at him. "I look forward to Tuesday."

"Me, too," Josh replied, also rising. "It was great meeting you, Amelia." After another shared smile, Josh headed off into the crowd.

"Let's go, handsome," Rigel urged, squeezing Tucker's hip. "I'm ready to go somewhere I can actually hold a conversation with you."

Tucker nodded, and they all headed toward the door. Once outside, Amelia headed left, while Rigel guided him toward the right. After the door closed behind them, blocking out most of the thumping of the music, Tucker tipped his head up and eyed Rigel.

"So, your name is Rigel?"

Rigel grinned at him. "Yeah. Rigel Patterson." Chuckling, he admitted, "Guess I should have told you that before." Rigel winked as he asked, "What about you, handsome? What's your name?"

"Tucker," he answered, uncomfortable giving out more to a one-night stand.

CHAPTER THREE

Rigel wanted to press for more, but he scented Tucker's discomfort. When he'd asked to take his mate home with him in the club, he'd smelled the same. Evidently, his human had had a poor experience with going home with someone.

I'll make it my mission to remove any doubt and to give my mate the best damn experience of his life. Then I'll figure out ways to top it.

With that plan in mind, Rigel squeezed Tucker's hip and led him to Dane's motorcycle. He felt damn grateful the fellow shifter had not only helped him regain his self-control while in the club but had offered his bike. The fellow enforcer loved his *Harley Electra Road Glide*, and Rigel could probably guess how many people he'd allowed to borrow it.

He knows the power of mates, though, but I definitely owe him one.

When Rigel stopped beside the powerful machine, Tucker gaped. "A motorcycle?" His expression showed clear disbelief, and he even took a small step backward. "When your friend offered his ride, I didn't realize this is what he meant."

Rigel tightened his hold before easing it. "I'll admit, it's been a few years since I've ridden, but I do know how to operate the machine," he assured, hoping to soothe Tucker. "I'll get us home safely."

As Rigel watched, Tucker swallowed hard. Rigel could practically see the wheels turning in his human's head. His soon-to-be lover definitely didn't have faith in him.

Deciding to offer a little encouragement while finding out

the problem, Rigel wrapped his arms around Tucker from behind. He cuddled against his human, nuzzling his nose and lips along the man's neck. His mouth watered with his desire to sink his canines in and mark his mate.

Resisting that urge, Rigel quietly asked, "Are you afraid of motorcycles, Tucker?" He pressed a kiss to the sensitive flesh behind his human's ear, enjoying the soft gasp his mate let out. "I would never put you in harms' way, my mate," Rigel assured. "You'll always be safe with me."

"N-Not afraid," Tucker told him, turning his head a little to peer over his shoulder at him. "But, um, I tasted the liquor on your tongue. You've been drinking."

"Before I came to the club, yes," Rigel admitted, understanding Tucker's concern. "But, please, trust me. I *am* sober."

Rigel couldn't very well tell him that his shifter metabolism processed alcohol damn fast. Even with what he'd drank at the restaurant, the second he'd scented Tucker and realized what it meant, any hint of being slightly drunk had burned from his system. The fifteen minutes it had taken Rigel to track Tucker down amidst the throngs of people at the club had been the longest of his life.

And now, I have him here in my arms and need to figure out how to get him into my home and my bed.

Tucker continued to hesitate.

"Let me take you home with me, Tucker," Rigel rumbled, easing his hands back under his mate's shirt. He teased his fingers over the lean lines of his belly with one hand while sliding the second up to flick a nipple with his thumb, pleased to feel it bead beneath his ministrations. Hearing Tucker gasp and feeling him push into him, Rigel continued, "I want to see you spread out on my bed, to kiss and lick every inch of your body, handsome. I wanna make you fly with pleasure. Please let me."

"O-Okay," Tucker replied, his voice husky, betraying his desire just as the thick aroma of his arousal did. Then he quickly added the caveat, "But only if there's helmets."

"Dane does," Rigel assured, doing a mental fist-pump. "They're locked in the saddlebags."

Rigel had seen Dane do it. While some states didn't require a helmet, Georgia did. Besides, he knew his fellow enforcer would never allow his human mate on his bike without one, regardless of the law.

"I'll get them."

Rigel did as he stated, although releasing Tucker was damn difficult. He loved feeling his mate in his arms. He never wanted to be without the man again.

All in good time.

After pulling out the helmets, Rigel placed Danny's on Tucker's head. He was glad it fit his mate, even though Dane's mate was a bit smaller than his own. Once Rigel had buckled the helmet, he quickly donned his own. Rigel also pulled out the men's leather motorcycle jackets and offered the smaller to Tucker, who took it without question. When Rigel pulled on Dane's, he was relieved it fit reasonably well even though the other enforcer was a bit larger than him.

Once Rigel had swung his leg over the motorcycle, he righted the bike. He held out his left hand, offering it to Tucker. To his pleasure, his mate only hesitated an instant before accepting and climbing onto the bike behind him.

Rigel waited until Tucker seemed to get comfortable behind him before firing up the motorcycle. Then he encouraged his mate to tighten his arms around his waist. Feeling his human's hold on him, Rigel smiled with pleasure as he started them moving.

The drive to Rigel's home was a new form of torture. He relished the heat of his human's back against his own. Every time he turned his head, Rigel could take in Tucker's delicious aroma, causing his balls to ache and his cock to throb. He couldn't recall the last time he'd felt such need.

While Rigel wished he could converse with Tucker, to get

to know his mate a little, the *Harley*'s loud engine wasn't conducive to talking. He figured Dane's helmets had speakers, but he didn't know how to use the function. Instead, Rigel used every stoplight and stop sign to squeeze Tucker's wrist or thigh. Rigel wanted his mate to get used to him touching him because he planned to do it often.

So much to explain to him . . . but after.

Finally, *finally*, Rigel reached the large bungalow he called home on the outskirts of Savannah. His place was situated in a community of fellow shifters with several acre lots and plenty of forest. Rigel's place was positioned at the edge of a marsh area, allowing him access to shift into his alligator form and enjoy the water.

"This is nice," Tucker murmured once Rigel had parked in front of his garage and shut off the engine.

"Thanks." Rigel twisted a bit to peer at Tucker. "It's been home for a few years, and I like it."

A few years was a bit of an understatement, but Rigel couldn't share that he'd been living there for nearly fifty years. He'd even *sold* it to his current identity nearly fifteen years before and had lived in seclusion for almost a decade, only interacting with fellow shifters. Rigel had appreciated being able to go back into human society nearly five years before. It'd been a good thing he'd been living so close to other shifters so he hadn't been truly isolated.

After swinging off the back of the motorcycle, Tucker turned his head, looking one way, then another. "Uh, secluded."

Once again, Rigel scented his mate's nerves. "It *is* secluded." As he removed the helmet and leather jacket, he grinned and waggled his brows. "I enjoy being nude quite a bit, so seclusion is necessary for me."

Rigel figured that was true from a certain point of view. Plus, once he convinced his mate to move in with him, he planned for them both to be naked . . . *a lot.*

After locking their borrowed items in the saddlebags, Rigel led the way to the detached, three-car garage. He punched in a code on the side, causing the large door to open. Then Rigel moved Dane's motorcycle into the empty bay he used to work on his own vehicles.

"Come on, Tucker," Rigel urged, taking his human's hand. As he led his mate back out of the garage and toward the house, he roved his gaze up and down the man's lean body that he couldn't wait to get his hands on. "Let's go get comfortable."

Tucker followed in silence, and Rigel could scent a mixture of anticipation, arousal, and a little worry.

That won't do.

Rigel unlocked his front door and stepped inside, closing them both inside. After hanging both his own keys and Dane's into a wall rack to the left of the door, he turned and slid his arm around Tucker's waist. Rigel threaded the fingers of his other hand into his beautiful human's sandy-blond hair and cradled his head.

"Now," Rigel rumbled, peering into Tucker's wide hazel eyes. "Where were we before we got interrupted?"

Without waiting for Tucker to respond, Rigel dipped his head and sealed his mouth over his human's. He nipped his bottom lip, then suckled the flesh. At the same time, Rigel slid his hand to the side a little, allowing him to press his thumb against the corner of Tucker's mouth, urging him to open. When his human obeyed, Rigel took complete advantage, thrusting his tongue in deep.

Mapping Tucker's mouth with his tongue, Rigel learned every bit of him. He basked in the masculine flavor of his soon-to-be lover, so deep and unique. Rigel thought Tucker tasted even better the second time around, and he knew he would never be able to get enough of the man in his arms.

The way Tucker clung to him, his fingers biting into the

flesh of his shoulders through Rigel's shirt, how he moaned wantonly as he kissed Rigel back, even how he pressed his whole body against Rigel's, possibly going onto his toes to do it—every response, every*thing* about his mate was just perfect.

Feeling the ridge of Tucker's erection pressing against his own each time his mate rocked against him caused Rigel to feed his mate a groan. The exquisite tingles shooting through his groin made his balls ache. His cock throbbed, twitching and leaking behind his fly.

When breathing became a necessity, Rigel tore his lips from Tucker's. He sucked in a much-needed lungful of air as he stared into his mate's flushed face. With his human's lips kiss-swollen and his eyes dilated with passion, Rigel knew he'd never seen a more riveting sight in his life.

"Gods, you're stunning," Rigel muttered huskily. Dipping his head, he pressed a chaste kiss to those swollen lips. "So fucking gorgeous." Turning his head, Rigel began trailing kisses along Tucker's jaw while muttering, "And mine. All mine. My mate."

When Rigel reached Tucker's neck, his mate tipped his chin up in such sweet submission. He groaned and latched his lips onto his forever love's smooth flesh. Sucking, licking, and nibbling, Rigel worked the flesh he longed to sink his canines into.

"No marks," Tucker whispered roughly.

That was something Rigel knew he could never agree to, but he didn't voice a counter. Instead, he nipped Tucker's flesh once more before lifting his head. He stared into his mate's face, pleased to see the glazed need darkening Tucker's hazel eyes nearly to brown.

"You're so fucking delectable, my mate," Rigel muttered, tightening the arm he had around Tucker's waist. He felt his mate's answering hardness against his own and rocked his hips. "So damn close already."

"M-Me, too," Tucker squeaked, bucking against him. "Shit!"

When Tucker tried to ease back, Rigel let him. "Time to take the edge off," he declared before dropping to his knees and reaching for his mate's fly. Rigel didn't bother asking for permission. He quickly undid Tucker's button and zipper as he murmured, "Can't wait to taste you."

Then Rigel pushed the jeans down with one hand while gripping Tucker's briefs with the other, moving them out of the way, too. The slender erection that sprang free was a thing of beauty. Rigel's mouth watered as he took in the swollen maybe seven-inch length.

A perfect mouthful.

With that thought, Rigel parted his lips and swallowed his mate's dick to the root. Tucker's masculine flavor burst across his tongue, and Rigel groaned with pleasure as it lit up his taste buds. Never had he experienced anything so exquisite, and he sucked hard as he drew partway off Tucker's prick before reversing and burying his nose in his lover's groin.

Oh-so-good.

"R-Rigel?"

Hearing his mate cry his name, listening to him groan as Rigel blew him, Rigel felt his own arousal soar. He moaned around his mouthful of meat, his cock throbbing in his jeans. As Rigel continued to service Tucker's slender rod, he scrambled to open his own jeans.

Rigel had just managed to yank open his fly when he felt Tucker pushing at his shoulder and whimpering. Ignoring the warning, he sank deep again. His mate barked a harsh cry, stiffened, and came, pouring his release down Rigel's throat.

Humming, Rigel backed off a little, eager for the next burst to land on his tongue. He wasn't disappointed, and he took a second to savor the slightly salty dollop of goodness before swallowing. When the third volley coated his taste buds, Rigel felt his balls pull tight, and he didn't even try to stop what was coming.

As Rigel continued to suckle on Tucker's dick, his orgasm washed over his senses. Pleasure burst through his system as his cock erupted untouched. His prick twitched and jerked as his seed spurted from him to land on the stone of his foyer.

Rigel wasn't certain how long he remained on his knees, his mate's dick resting in his mouth, before he came back to his senses. Opening eyes he couldn't remember closing, he peered up at Tucker as he straightened, releasing his still half-hard flesh. Licking his lips, Rigel enjoyed the traces of seed still on his lips as he took in his human's flushed, sated expression and glazed eyes.

"Damn," Rigel murmured with a grin, sitting back on his thighs. "That's a fantastic look on you, my mate."

"Y-You've called me that a f-few times," Tucker mumbled, blinking slowly, obviously trying to pull himself together. "Why?"

Oops.

Rigel knew it wasn't the time to explain, so he shrugged and stated, "Term of endearment, handsome." Then he rubbed his palms up Tucker's bare upper thighs and teased his thumbs along the edges of his mate's pubic hair. "Ready to move this to the bedroom for round two?"

Tucker furrowed his eyebrows as he stared down at him. "Round two?"

Nodding, Rigel rose to his feet, unmindful of his drooping jeans. "That was just to take the edge off." He teased his fingertip around the edge of Tucker's lips. "I'm still going to explore every inch of your body and make love to you, Tucker."

After clearing his throat, Tucker pulled his underwear and jeans back up his legs before stating, "Then you better show me to your bedroom."

More than on board with that, Rigel gripped the waist of

his jeans in one hand and wrapped his other arm around Tucker's waist. He guided his mate to his bedroom.

At long last.

CHAPTER FOUR

"Sooooo."

Tucker looked up from the loan application form he'd been processing to see Amelia leaning a hip against his desk. Glancing toward the door, he appreciated the fact that she'd closed it. Still, he noticed it wasn't locked.

Not surprising. If Dad came across a locked office door, he'd immediately start knocking . . . and then ask too many questions.

Neither of them wanted that.

Arching one brow at her, Tucker asked, "Yeah?"

Amelia's smile turned knowing. "You didn't call me." Fortunately, she kept her voice low. "How did it go with your hottie?"

Thinking of his evening before with Rigel, Tucker had to bite back a moan. The man had lived up to every promise he'd made. Tucker's body had sung from his exploratory mouth, tongue, and hands. He'd even passed out after the second round of fucking.

Creeping out of Rigel's home in the wee hours of the morning had been the hardest thing Tucker had ever done. His one-night stand had turned out to be a damn insatiable lover. Tucker couldn't remember the last time he'd gotten off three times within a few hours.

On top of that, Rigel had ended up being a cuddler.

When Tucker had woken up wrapped in Rigel's arms, he'd worried he wouldn't be able to slip away from the bigger man's hold. As it was, it had taken a little work . . . and patience. Tucker had wanted to stay in the handsome man's hold forever . . . but no way did he want to brave the walk of shame in front of him in the morning.

To that end, Tucker had managed to slip free of Rigel's hold. He'd crept around the room, gathered his stuff, and carried everything to the front room. Then he'd dressed and called for a cab, using a piece of mail on the front room stand to give them an address.

Tucker had waited at the end of the long driveway.

"Well?"

Snapping his attention to Amelia and away from his very pleasant memories, Tucker smiled at his sister. "Thanks for going with me to the club last night. It was just the kind of fun I needed for the night."

Shoving down the heat that threatened his cheeks, Tucker tried to focus on the paperwork he still needed to finish. There was someone waiting, after all. Hoping to get her to back off, Tucker tossed her question back at her.

"So?" Tucker flung at Amelia before refocusing on his typing. "What about you?" He paused to smirk up at her. "Josh?"

"Josh and I have a date on Tuesday, remember?" Amelia then pinned him with a narrow-eyed gaze. "And you are so not getting away with telling me nothing," she declared, crossing her arms over her chest and frowning. "At least tell me if he was good or not."

Tucker knew that if he wanted Amelia to back off, he would have to give her at least a little. He just wasn't certain what to tell her. Tucker hesitated a few seconds, then admitted, "He rocked my world."

Amelia squealed softly and did a tiny happy dance as she grinned widely at him. "So?" She glanced toward the door, obviously just as nervous as Tucker to be talking about him being with a man while at work with their father somewhere around. Still, Amelia lowered her voice and persisted, "Are you going to see him again? What's his name?"

"His name's Rigel, and no." Admitting that caused a touch of sadness to slither through Tucker.

"Why not?" Amelia looked at him aghast. "What aren't you telling me?"

"He was a one-night stand," Tucker reminded her, keeping his voice low. "We were both at that club for the same reason. A pick-up."

Tucker purposefully tried to forget all the times Rigel called him mine and claimed they were meant for each other. It would have been so wonderful to be true, but Tucker knew better than to believe in words issued during the heat of sex.

"Did you offer your number and he refused?"

With a sigh, Tucker shook his head. His sister was always a romantic. She believed he could get his happily-ever-after with whoever he wanted.

Life didn't work that way, though.

Pointing toward the door, Tucker stated, "Have you forgotten that we both work for Father, and we both know his opinions on many things, including gays."

In truth, his father was pretty much an equal-opportunity bigot, but he sure put on a good face at the dealership. When dealing with customers, he treated everyone with courtesy because he wanted their money. The lure of the almighty dollar bill held his father's tongue and attitude in check until the contract was signed and the person was driving away in their new car.

Then Tucker and Amelia got to hear all about the person's faults—too fat, too thin, a woman dressed as a slut, a Black person, a Hispanic person, an old man with a comb-over. Everyone was fair game.

"Can you imagine if I dated a guy and he found out?" Tucker shook his head and grimaced even as he wondered what it would be like to spend more time with Rigel. "Dad would shit purple kittens and fire me on the spot, then black-ball me from the car industry."

Amelia nibbled her bottom lip. Her expression said she wanted to counter Tucker, but she didn't. That was just the cold hard truth.

Tucker had always worked sales for his father's car dealer-ship. Growing up, it had been expected that he would join the family business after high school. He'd taken business and marketing courses in college but hadn't finished his degree because their business had picked up and his father had wanted him to work full-time.

"Well, that's just stupid," Amelia finally grumbled with a sigh. "And I'm sorry."

Tucker shrugged. "Not your fault." Then he pointed to-ward the door. "Best get back out there." Amelia handled the phones and administration. Forcing a smile, Tucker added, "Besides, I swing both ways, remember? Someday, I'm sure I'll find some nice girl I can bring home to Mother."

Amelia and a couple of Tucker's friends were the only peo-ple that knew of his bisexuality. He kept that part of himself far, *far* away from his parents.

As Amelia muttered, "You should be able to love who you want," and started toward the door, Tucker silently agreed. He thought about finding some girl to love, but the image of a naked Rigel mapping his body with his hands and tongue flashed into his mind. His blood heated in his veins, and he felt himself begin to stiffen behind the fly of his slacks.

Shoving those thoughts away, Tucker did his best to refo-cus on his work. He feared that Rigel had ruined him for any other. Just the idea of touching someone else — or having them touch him — caused his stomach to churn.

Tucker lifted his hand to where his neck met his shoulder but hesitated to touch. Even though Tucker had warned him not to leave a mark, the big man hadn't listened. At some point during their encounter, Rigel had bitten him . . . hard.

Instead of hurting him, Tucker had been sent into orbit. His body had orgasmed even though he'd come just a few seconds before. He hadn't asked about it at the time, but when he'd arrived home and discovered what looked like a small scar, he'd felt a flash of anger at the audacity of the man.

Then Tucker had touched it. His blood had fired through his veins, and images of everything he still wanted to do to and with Rigel had cascaded through his brain. Tucker had even hurried to the shower and rubbed one out.

What would it be like to have Rigel focused on my pleasure on a regular basis?

Guess I'll never know.

With that depressing thought in mind, Tucker felt his flash of arousal die a quick death.

For the best.

Tucker forced himself to get back to work. His customer wanted to buy a slightly used *Honda*, and he intended to make it happen. Too bad the guy's credit rating wasn't all that good, but Tucker still hoped he could work some magick.

"Hey, Tucker. Still hard at it?"

Upon hearing his father's voice in the doorway, Tucker looked up from his computer. "Yes, sir," he replied with a glance at his screen before refocusing on his father. "Just about finished."

"Good, good." Tucker's father—Gary Rolden—cut a fine figure in his suit. Even at fifty-eight years old, he kept himself in great shape. "Did you have a good birthday outing with your sister yesterday? She said you all went dancing at some club." As Tucker forced down his desire to blush upon thinking about his time at the club, his father continued with, "You know you're never going to find a nice girl in a place like that."

Just that fast, Tucker's urge to blush was gone. "I don't know, Father," he replied, unable to help himself from diverting his attention. "Amelia got a date out of it, so maybe there are some good ones there after all." When Tucker saw his father's eyes narrow, he mentally reminded himself that he was never supposed to counter his father's opinion, and he hurried to add, "But I did have a good time, thanks. A night dancing and a few drinks were just the thing."

Gary stared at him for several heartbeats, and Tucker feared his father would decide to ask for specifics. Fortunately, he didn't. Instead, he stated, "Well, sorry we couldn't meet up for dinner on your birthday, but you know every third Friday night is poker night with my friends."

"I know, sir," Tucker replied, forcing a smile. Of course his father wouldn't skip poker for his son's birthday. "It's no problem." Wanting out of the conversation, Tucker added, "I look forward to dinner with you and Mom tomorrow evening. I love that Italian place."

As they were gathering to celebrate Tucker's birthday, he'd been the one to choose the restaurant. That was a tradition that he intended to continue if he ever had a family. Whoever was having the birthday chose the place they ate at.

Good thing, too, or Tucker would never get his father there.

Considering the slight curl of his lip, Tucker readied himself for something derogatory. "Well, it's your birthday," his father muttered instead. Then he followed up by saying, "And I was going to talk to you about that. We're going to need to move the meet-up time to about two in the afternoon, instead of dinner at six."

"Really?" Tucker blurted the question before he could think better of it. "Why?"

Gary shoved his hands into his trouser pockets as he began to turn away. "My friend, Lloyd, and his wife invited your mother and me to a function at the country club, so we'll need to be done with dinner early enough to get to that." Then his father strode from the room, calling over his shoulder, "Enjoy your Saturday night, son."

Tucker sat there for several long minutes, staring at the empty doorway where his father had disappeared. There were so many times when he wondered about his father's attitude and behavior. While Tucker was growing up, Gary had never been a warm man, but the older Tucker became, the more selfish his father's actions seemed to become.

Maybe not having him in my life if I find a male partner wouldn't be such a bad thing.

Instantly, Tucker's thoughts returned to Rigel. He lifted a hand and touched where the scar was hidden beneath his shirt and tie. Zings of awareness still traveled through his body, as if the mark had suddenly become an erogenous zone.

"One-night stand," Tucker muttered, shaking his head.

Even with that thought in mind, as Tucker finished his work, he wondered what Rigel was doing right then. Had he been sorry to see him gone in the morning? Or had he been grateful he hadn't had to boot him?

Shaking his head, Tucker knew he would never get the answers to those questions.

"Hey, you hear about the time change to your birthday meal, then?"

Tucker turned to see Amelia in the doorway. She stood with her arms crossed over her breasts while leaning one shoulder against the doorframe. Her right foot remained on the floor, but she'd pulled her left foot from her high heel and was rubbing the ball of that foot against her right calf. Tucker had seen that move plenty of times, telling him that she was more than ready to be out of those shoes.

He still didn't understand why his father insisted she wear business attire and heels.

"Yeah, I heard," Tucker confirmed, hitting submit on the

document he'd just finished. "For a damn country club function."

"I swear he wasn't always like this, was he?" Amelia voiced Tucker's own thoughts from earlier, sounding just as confused. "It's like he . . ." Her voice trailed off as if she were searching for the right words.

"Yeah, I know what you mean," Tucker told her, rising. His chute twinged as he moved, reminding him of Rigel and their night together. Tucker clenched his muscles, just to enjoy the sensation again. Realizing what he did, he cleared his throat and grabbed his suit jacket from the back of his chair. "Ready to lock up?"

Amelia swept her gaze over him, and she narrowed her eyes. "Thinking of a certain someone?"

Draping his jacket over his arm, Tucker muttered, "I don't want to talk about it."

"You really like him," Amelia countered. "I can tell." She fell into step beside Tucker as they started making the rounds, making certain all the other employees had left and everything was locked up. "You know where he lives. Drop by." When Tucker stubbornly remained silent, Amelia nudged him with her elbow. "How will you know if you don't try?"

"One-night stand, remember?"

As Tucker said the words, he began to wonder if he was reminding her . . . or himself.

CHAPTER FIVE

Rigel knew his house was empty even as he eased from his bed. Pain knifed through his chest as he felt the sheets next to him. They were cold.

When did my mate slip away? Why?

While Rigel knew he hadn't explained a damn thing to his human, he thought he'd called him mine and shared how perfect they were together enough times that Tucker wouldn't think it was a one-night stand. Evidently, Rigel hadn't been clear enough.

How could I have slept so hard that I missed Tucker leaving the bed?

Rigel didn't know, but he suspected it was a mixture of the adrenaline crash from finding his mate coupled with several fantastic orgasms. Maybe it was his imagination, but he thought he could still taste Tucker's flavor on his tongue. His cum had been nearly as delicious as the sweet iron-rich nectar flowing through his mate's veins.

Even as Rigel stalked through the quiet house searching for Tucker—just in case—his morning wood stiffened with need for the other half of his soul. He remembered the exquisite feel of his mate's chute muscles wrapped around his length. If it weren't for the condom he'd agreed to wear, Rigel would have fully bonded them. He'd just been too eager, too excited, to resist the allure of Tucker's neck.

With them partially bonded, Rigel knew that Tucker would soon be missing him just as badly as Rigel missed his mate. His human just wouldn't understand the compulsion he was feeling to return to him. Rigel didn't want to cause his mate any discomfort so that meant tracking him down.

Except, I don't know his last name.

Hell, Rigel barely knew anything about Tucker at all. He had a first name, a scent, and a face. Rigel scrubbed his fingers through his hair in frustration as he realized he had no clue how to go about finding his mate.

"I thought I'd have time to talk to him this morning," Rigel muttered to himself, knowing he'd allowed his dick to do the thinking last night. "Now what?"

Standing in the middle of the empty living room, Rigel inhaled deeply. The scent of his mate was faint, telling him that Tucker must have snuck out hours before . . . well before first light. Rigel growled under his breath, his alligator rumbling irritably in agreement.

They both wanted their mate.

"Okay. Think." Rigel closed his eyes and tipped his head back, trying to come up with some solution. "A name and a face." Then it hit him. "And the location where I met him has cameras."

While Rigel wasn't the most tech-savvy person around, he had friends who were. Pivoting, he rushed back to his bedroom. Grabbing his phone from the nightstand, Rigel dialed a number. As Rigel waited for his friend to answer, he began to pace his large master bedroom, inhaling deeply, enjoying the lingering smell of his and Tucker's exploits. His cock, which had softened upon finding his mate gone, began to swell once more.

Shit!

"I didn't think you'd come up for air for at least two days." Link's teasing voice came through the line. "Need me to cover a shift at headquarters today or something?"

"I need help, but not with that." Rigel had the day off, which was why he'd been willing to cut a little loose the prior evening. "My mate is gone."

"Your mate is gone?" Link responded incredulously. "What the fuck did you do, Rigel?"

"It's what I didn't do," Rigel admitted, plopping onto the bed with a groan. "We didn't, uh, talk much." Resting his head in his hand, he mumbled, "Or at all, really."

"Oh, fuck," Link muttered. His deep sigh came through the line before he guessed. "So he thought it was a one-night stand and skedaddled."

"Yeah," Rigel confirmed, his voice gruff with frustration. "While I was sleeping."

Gods. How embarrassing. I finally find my mate and lose him just as quickly.

No. No, damn it. Don't think like that.

"Okay, okay. Take a deep breath in, then let it out slowly," Link crooned softly. "Try not to panic, man. We'll find him."

Rigel didn't know how his friend knew he was coming unglued, but he followed his directions anyway. After blowing out one breath, then two, he no longer felt as if he was going to panic. Rubbing his forehead, Rigel did his best to remain focused on Tucker's delicious scent lingering in the bedroom.

Mmmm . . . so good.

"You with me, Rigel?"

Lifting his head from the pillow Tucker had used, Rigel rolled onto his back. "Yeah." He wasn't even certain when he'd flopped over and pushed his nose into the fabric. "I'm okay."

"Okay, well." Link didn't sound convinced. "I asked for your mate's name. When Dane came and told us, he said he hadn't heard it, yet."

"Tucker." Rigel smiled as he thought of his handsome mate's name. It was a perfect name for his sexy human. "His name is Tucker."

"Tucker what?"

Rigel winced as he admitted, "I don't know."

"You don't know?" Link's surprise came through loud and

clear. "You didn't ask your mate's surname? What about his phone number?"

"No," Rigel whined. "I just . . . I got my hands and mouth on him and—" He sighed, his mouth watering for another taste of Tucker.

"Well, shit." Link heaved a deep sigh. "Now I know why he thought he was a one-night stand."

"I know. *Fuck!*"

"Come down to Shifter Headquarters," Link ordered. "I'll hack into the DMV and begin a search for any driver's licenses with the name Tucker."

Hope filled Rigel.

"At the same time, I'll look at video footage from last night at *The Amnesty*," Link continued. "I'll need you to look at it and spot your mate. That way, I can match it to any DMV pictures that pop up." The sound of keys clicking came through the line, telling Rigel that his buddy was getting started. "Then I can run a facial rec on social media and see if anything pops there, too."

"Yeah, yeah," Rigel replied excitedly, popping up from the bed. "Anything I can do to help."

"Don't get your hopes too high just yet, Rigel," Link warned. "There are millions of people living in the state and over a hundred thousand in Savannah alone. This could take some time." His next words were muttered, as if he wasn't really talking to Rigel anymore. "That's if he's even from this state. Hope to hell he isn't just visiting from somewhere."

Wincing, Rigel mentally agreed. "I'll be there as soon as I can."

"See you," Link mumbled before disconnecting the line.

Rigel nearly skipped the shower, considering he liked having Tucker's scent on his skin. Except, he smelled like sex, too, and going to Shifter Headquarters stinking to high heaven wasn't the politest thing to do. As loath as he was to wash away most of Tucker's scent—it would take several to get rid of all of it, and he planned to find his mate before the day's end—Rigel hopped in the shower and gave his body a perfunctory scrubbing.

Hmmm . . . how would it be to have Tucker in here with me? Wet and soapy.

At his thoughts, Rigel's cock began to thicken anew.

Shit. Focus. Find my mate and actually fucking talk to him.

With that thought in mind, Rigel turned off the water and grabbed a towel.

After dressing, Rigel headed toward the front door. He spotted Dane's motorcycle keys hanging there and nearly decided to use the man's bike again. Rigel could reminisce about how it felt to have Tucker's arms around his waist.

Instead, Rigel grabbed his truck's keys and shot off a text to Dane about where and when he would want to get his motorcycle. Of course, that caused the fellow enforcer to text him back, teasing him about worrying about his bike when he was with his mate. When Rigel texted back that Tucker wasn't with him anymore, he got a phone call.

Rigel switched Dane's call to Bluetooth so he could drive and ended up with a-whole-nother round of ribbing as well as a promise to help in any way he could.

"You're hovering, Rigel," Link grumbled, not looking away from his computer screen. "Why don't you get out of here for a while?"

"And do what?" Rigel snapped, pacing Link's large computer room. He thrust his fingers through his hair, yanking it free of the ponytail he'd had it in. "My fucking mate is out there somewhere. I need to find him."

The last twenty-four-plus hours had been the longest of Rigel's life. It had taken him watching a good two hours of footage for him to spot Tucker on the club's feed. They'd tried to get a picture of him exiting with Rigel first, but due to the way he'd been holding Tucker, there hadn't been a clear shot. That meant they'd had to look for when he'd entered or inside the club.

Then, true to Link's concern, wading through Tuckers at the DMV was a slow process. Evidently, it was a fairly popular name. That was assuming he was even a registered driver in Georgia.

Rigel felt as if his life was on hold as his friends helped him sift for a needle in the proverbial haystack.

"Hey, Rigel," Dane greeted, entering the room. "Time to get some fresh air." He gripped Rigel's upper arm and began tugging him toward the door. "There's nothing for you to do in here but get worked up." When Rigel opened his mouth to protest, Dane countered, "Let Link do his work. He can text you pictures just as easily as you looking over his shoulder."

Even though Rigel didn't want to agree, he nodded and allowed Dane to pull him from the room. His friend was right, after all. Plus, pissing off his computer-savvy buddy wasn't a smart thing to do.

"Thanks, Dane," Link called without looking up.

"Thanks for texting, man," Dane responded, telling Rigel why the Komodo dragon shifter had shown up. "I'll keep him busy for a while."

Rigel strode beside Dane and realized the other enforcer was leading him toward the parking garage. "Where are we going?"

"When was the last time you ate?"

Hesitating, Rigel tried to recall.

"Yep, that's what I thought," Dane replied with an understanding smile. "But once we find Tucker, you're going to need your strength to woo him." With a scoff, he added, "And a hungry shifter is never a good thing."

"True," Rigel conceded, climbing into the passenger side of Dane's SUV. "Where are we going?"

"Someplace casual," Dane told him, glancing at him critically. "Because I have a funny feeling you haven't changed or showered since yesterday morning."

Rigel looked down at himself and winced. "Yeah. Was up all night pacing," he admitted.

Dane patted him on the shoulder before turning the SUV out of the underground parking garage. "We'll get you fed, then take you out for a swim." Flashing an encouraging smile Rigel's way, Dane told him, "That'll help you relax."

As a Komodo dragon shifter, Dane's animal was just as comfortable in the water as he was on land. Rigel had often played aquatic tag with him and his brothers. Well, with Dakota, anyway. It was rare that Delanrue's animal felt that sociable.

Although, not as rare now that he's bonded with Miggs.

The cute little guinea pig shifter had really helped Delanrue to relax and loosen up.

When Dane pulled into the parking lot, Rigel recognized the place. It was owned by an older couple and boasted authentic Italian cuisine. The place was a little rundown but still clean. Plus, the dishes were large, and the food delicious.

Rigel exited the vehicle, and as soon as the scent of the food hit his stomach, it rumbled.

Dane chuckled and patted him on the shoulder. "Come on. A couple of the other guys are meeting us here."

Nodding, Rigel strode toward the door. Dane reached it first and opened it for him. He headed inside and turned toward the bar area, spotting Del already sitting there. Rigel's boss, Mycroft, was there, too, as was Mycroft's vampire mate, Boyd.

Opening his mouth, Rigel lifted a hand in preparation for a greeting. The sound of a smooth tenor man talking caused him to freeze. He gasped as he jerked to the left, searching for the speaker.

It can't be . . . can it?

Except, it was.

Sitting at a square table for four was Tucker.

"My mate," Rigel whispered, shocked beyond reason.

Dane's hand landed on Rigel's shoulder and squeezed in encouragement. "We'll find him, Rigel," he rumbled softly into his ear. "I promise we won't stop looking."

"No." Rigel lifted his hand and pointed, unable to stop the way it trembled. "My mate is here." Out of the corner of his eye, Rigel noticed Dane follow where he pointed. "Tucker's here."

"Well, fuck, man," Dane murmured, sounding just as surprised. "Damn, Fate is good to you." With a low chuckle, his buddy asked, "Want me to order you somethin' while you go say hi?"

"Yeah." Even though eating was the last thing on his mind, Rigel felt his stomach ache from emptiness. He really did need sustenance. "Um, be right there?"

"Take your time, man," Dane encouraged. Then he squeezed Rigel's upper arm until he focused on the other enforcer. Dane's brown eyes held a wealth of warning. "Make a good impression this time, huh?"

Rigel nodded. "Right."

After Dane released him, Rigel took a few deep breaths to try to center himself before he started toward Tucker. He knew his mate was sitting with his sister, Amelia. Rigel recognized her from the club. He would guess the older pair were their parents, but he only had eyes for Tucker. Roving his gaze over Tucker, Rigel couldn't believe how fast his heart pounded at once again being in his presence. The closer he drew to the table, the stronger his lover's exquisite scent became, flooding his senses.

By the time Rigel reached Tucker's table, his mouth was watering to taste his human, and his arms ached to hold him close. "Tucker," he rasped, his voice deep with his need.

Tucker turned his head and looked up at him. His hazel eyes widened as recognition filled his expression. For an instant, desire flashed within the depths of his human's eyes before his mate tempered the response and uncertainty replaced it.

That wouldn't do at all.

Gripping Tucker's upper arm, Rigel urged his mate to his feet, who probably came willingly due to shock. That was fine. A second later, Rigel had Tucker right where he wanted him . . . in his arms again.

"You fucking left me," Rigel grumbled, threading his fingers through Tucker's hair. "Never again."

Then, unable to control his need a second longer, Rigel gave in to temptation and sealed his mouth over Tucker's. Just as two days prior, when his mate's flavor burst across his taste buds, the rest of the world melted away. Rigel didn't remember they were in a public restaurant. All that mattered was that Tucker was in his arms again.

That was until a deep voice shouted, "What the fuck?"

Tucker jerked his head back with a gasp, ending the kiss. His face flushed, but not from pleasure. Instead, fear permeated his scent as he looked toward the red-faced man standing beside the table.

"No son of mine is a fucking faggot," the man roared.

Rigel felt the tremble work through his mate's body, and realization hit him.

His mate wasn't out.

Well, shit.

CHAPTER SIX

Oh fuck! Oh fuck! Oh fuck!

Tucker was pretty sure he'd just had his best fantasy and his worst nightmare clash. When he'd looked up and seen Rigel standing there, staring down at him with possessive heat in his dark eyes, he'd thought he'd been dreaming. After all, Rigel had dominated his dreams most of the night.

Then when Rigel had pulled him to his feet, wrapped his arms around him, and begun kissing him to within an inch of his life, Tucker had realized it wasn't a dream. He'd also been helpless to stop himself from kissing the big man back. There was just something about Rigel, some sort of animal magnetism that Tucker lost himself in.

Just like in the club, the world around Tucker had melted away . . . until his father's shout.

Upon seeing Gary Rolden's expression, Tucker knew what was coming. He hadn't any delusions that his father would be understanding. It wouldn't matter that they were in a restaurant or that they were there celebrating Tucker's birthday. His father was just as livid as he'd feared he would be if he ever discovered his son liked men.

And to find out like this?

"Are you tellin' me you're a fuckin' faggot, boy?" his father raged, his face red and his dark eyes promising retribution if Tucker didn't say the right thing. He waved a thick finger between them. "That what this display is for? To tell me you're a fuckin' queer?"

"No, sir," Tucker whispered. Feeling Rigel's arms still

around him and the hand that had been in his hair having been moved to his upper arm, Tucker didn't miss the way the big man tensed, clinging to him just a little bit tighter. Tucker also couldn't deny just how right it felt to be there in Rigel's hold, either, and he blurted out, "I'm bi."

"You're mine, Tucker," Rigel declared gruffly. He glared at Tucker's father. "Don't you fuckin' talk to Tucker that way."

"I'll talk to my fuckin' son any way I want," his father shot right back. Then he curled his lip as he eyed them both. "Then again, maybe I don't have a son. Certainly no son of mine would do somethin' as unnatural as lie with a man." He gripped his mother's upper arm — who still sat wide-eyed and pale at the table — and dragged her to her feet. "Come on, Nancy. We're leaving." Then his father scowled at Amelia. "Get up, daughter. Time to leave the presence of these abominations."

Amelia winced, but she did as she was told. Tucker knew that neither of them were ready to go against their father, no matter how much they disagreed with his views. Hell, both their jobs were dependent on their father.

As Amelia passed, she mouthed, "I'm sorry."

Tucker shuddered, thinking that would be it. Except his father turned back to offer one more parting shot. "Better get your head on straight, boy." Sneering, his dark eyes glittering with disgust, his father declared, "Your family and job or your deviant lifestyle." Then he stormed out of the restaurant, hauling a silently crying wife behind him.

"I'm so sorry, Tucker," Rigel rumbled, sounding contrite. He rubbed a hand up and down Tucker's spine, obviously attempting to soothe, but Tucker was too shocked for it to help. "I'm here for you, baby," Rigel continued softly. "You're not alone. You're mine, and I'll help any way I can."

Finally, Tucker snapped out of it and glared up at Rigel, the man who'd just made a hell of a mess out of his life. "I'm *yours?*" He scoffed as he jerked out of his grip. "Listen up, you possessive asshole. We had one night together." Tucker lifted a finger to indicate one ... and he couldn't help but have it be the middle one. "Get the fuck over yourself."

Tucker began pulling cash from his wallet. Their food was only half-eaten, but he wasn't going to stiff the owners because of their drama. After plopping a couple of hundreds onto the table—Tucker always kept a little on him for emergencies—he rushed from the restaurant.

Ignoring Rigel's call, as well as the pleading in his tone and expression, was far more difficult than Tucker thought it should have been. As he exited, his sister passed him, heading back inside. "Forgot my purse," she muttered. Giving him a tight smile, she added, "We'll get through this, brother."

Even as Tucker nodded and whispered, "Thanks," he spotted his father standing by their car, watching.

Leaving it at that, Tucker hurried to his hatchback, hitting the fob to unlock it on the way. After climbing behind the wheel, Tucker quickly started the car and locked the doors. He gripped the wheel tightly with both hands and tried to breathe deeply, knowing he needed to quell the shudders working through him before he could safely drive.

Tucker lifted his attention back to the restaurant, and his heart skipped a beat in his chest. Rigel stood just outside the door, his hands shoved into the pockets of his jeans. That was when Tucker noticed the way Rigel's dark hair hung around his face and how there appeared to be shadows under his eyes as if he hadn't slept.

His friend from the club—Dane—stood beside him, his hand on Tucker's shoulder, perhaps to keep him from coming after him.

Tucker blew out a breath, swallowed hard, and put his car in gear. Without another look at the restaurant, he drove away. When Tucker reached his apartment complex, he was a little surprised to see his sister's car already parked in the visitor's section.

How did she beat me?

Shaking his head as he parked, Tucker figured he must have been extra cautious driving. He shut off his engine and climbed out. By the time he shut the door, he saw Amelia already running toward him. Tucker had just enough presence of mind to open his arms and slide a foot back so he could keep his balance before she plowed into him, wrapping him in a tight hug.

"I'm so sorry that happened, Tuck," Amelia cried, squeezing him hard. Easing her grip a little, she leaned back and met his gaze. "I never thought he would be that bad." Furrowing her brows, Amelia shook her head. "I mean, maybe rant a little, but to give you an ultimatum?"

Tucker sighed, sadness filling him. "I knew he'd be that bad, Amelia," he admitted. Peering off to the left, he didn't really see the apartments, his attention fixed firmly in his memory. "He's always made nasty comments about homosexuality, but his bigotedness has really expanded in recent years."

"What are you going to do?" Amelia sounded worried. "You're not really going to give up that hottie for Dad, are you?"

Opening his mouth, Tucker paused. His words stuck in his throat. His brain froze. He couldn't remember the last time he'd felt such indecision.

"I mean, that kiss he laid on you was super *hawt*," Amelia commented with a giggle as she drew away from Tucker. She took his hand and began leading him toward his apartment. Then her tone turned musing. "Although, his claiming *you're mine* was a little concerning. Possessive much?"

Tucker nodded absently, having thought the same thing. After unlocking his door, he let Amelia in first. He felt the hairs on his neck stand on end and paused to look behind him.

For a few seconds, Tucker looked over the area, but he didn't see anyone who might have been focused on him.

With a sigh, Tucker headed inside, closing and locking the door behind him.

Amelia sat on the sofa, her feet tucked under her. "Do you want to talk about it?"

Crossing to the kitchen, Tucker opened his fridge and grabbed a couple of beers. "Honestly? No." He held one out toward her questioningly. "I don't work tomorrow. I want to order pizza"—he'd barely had the chance to touch his meal before Rigel had shown up—"get shit-faced, and not think about how my life just imploded."

After a few seconds of hesitation, Amelia nodded slowly. "Okay." She eyed the offered drink critically. "If that's what you want, we can do that. But unlike you, I do have to work tomorrow, so I'll take a soda." With a grimace, she added, "And I'll let you know how Father's acting tomorrow so you can be prepared for Tuesday."

"Thanks." Tucker gave Amelia her requested soda before sitting on the other end of the sofa. He took a deep swig of his beer, wondering what his work life would be like come Tuesday.

In the end, Tucker didn't have to wonder. The following morning, he received a text message—a fucking text message—from his father. It was short and sweet.

Take the week off to make your decision. I know you'll do the proper thing.

Tucker wondered if he would go out of his mind without anything to do but housework for a whole week. Just as quickly, another thought popped into his brain.

I bet Rigel could keep me plenty busy.

With a groan, Tucker rested his head in his hands and wondered what the fuck to do.

"That was the opposite of a good impression," Delanrue muttered, frowning at Rigel. "What the hell were you thinking?"

"Yeah, man." Dane shook his head, his hand on Rigel's shoulder the only thing keeping him from going after Tucker. "What the hell was up with all the *you're mine* crap?" The larger enforcer began to guide Rigel toward his SUV. Lowering his voice, Dane muttered, "He's fucking human. He doesn't know what that means."

"I smelled his scent again after missing him for over a day, and I . . . I just lost control," Rigel admitted. He had absolutely no excuse for his actions except that. "I never meant to hurt him by outing him to his father." Rubbing the back of his neck, he didn't comment when Delanrue opened the passenger door for him. "I didn't know they didn't know. I mean, his sister knew, so—" Rigel paused, shrugging helplessly. "Shit." Dejectedly, he climbed into the vehicle. Resting his head in his hands, he muttered, "What the fuck do I do now?"

"We're going back to headquarters," Dane told him as Delanrue climbed into the back seat. Arching a brow, he smirked at his older brother. "Need a ride, Del?"

Delanrue jerked a nod. "I came with Mycroft and Boyd." Waving a hand to indicate the large SUV, he stated, "Your backseat is bigger."

Dane barked a laugh before closing Rigel's door.

Reaching forward, Delanrue rested his hand on Rigel's shoulder. "Fate brought you to your mate again, Rigel. Have faith." A low growl filled his tone as he continued, "And remember, your mate will need you in these troubled times."

"Look on the bright side," Dane commented, climbing behind the wheel. "At least now you know his phone number." Giving him an encouraging smile, the other enforcer added, "And it seems you have an ally in his sister. She's the one who gave it to you, after all."

Rigel nodded, his unease backing off a bit at that reminder. Under the guise of having forgotten her purse, Amelia had returned to the table. She'd handed him a piece of paper as well as a bit of advice.

"Give Tucker a chance to calm down, Rigel," Amelia had told him. "This is a big upset, but he really likes you." She'd held his gaze steadily and warned, "But if you're not serious about him, back away right now."

"I'm serious about him," Rigel has responded. Then he'd added, "He's going to be my everything."

Amelia had nodded once, picked up her purse, and rushed from the restaurant.

"Also, we have his license plate number," Dane pointed out. "We'll give that to Link, and he'll be able to tell us everything about your mate in no time."

Heartened, Rigel nodded. Then his stomach rumbled, and he grimaced. Dane laughed, and Delanrue smirked.

"Don't worry, Rigel." Dane flashed a grin in his direction. "Mycroft changed our meals *to go*. He and Boyd will bring them soon."

"What'd you order for me?" Rigel asked absently, staring at the phone number written on the slip of paper Amelia had given him. He had it memorized after just one look, but seeing the physical paper settled something inside him. He had a point of contact for his mate.

"Does it matter?" Dane asked with a smirk.

Rigel shrugged. "Not really." He would eat tree bark right about then. "Just something to think about other than the look of hurt on Tucker's face and the scent of his fear."

Recalling those, Rigel felt as if someone was stabbing him in the gut.

"Meatball subs, shrimp linguini, chicken linguini, spaghetti with meatballs, fried calamari, shrimp scampi, and three side orders of meatballs."

Jerking his attention to Dane, Rigel arched one brow. "Is there anything you didn't order?"

Dane grinned at him. "The artichoke dip." He made a face. "Yuck."

Rigel thought that sounded pretty good right then. His stomach grumbled again.

Yep, I'm damn hungry.

Having seen his mate again, even after the shitty circumstances, Rigel found his appetite had returned in spades. He felt his alligator rumble in his mind and assured his beast that they would eat soon. While he did that, he intended to make a plan on how to woo his mate.

There must be some way I can make it up to him.

"Well, this explains the father's comment about losing his job," Delanrue snarled, curling his lip as he eyed Link's computer screen. "Tucker works for the asshole. Gary Rolden, it says."

"Damn," Rigel snapped, rubbing the back of his neck. "We all know that it's not legal to fire someone for their sexual orientation, but that doesn't mean the bastard won't come up with some other excuse." Picking up a shrimp scampi, Rigel asked, "Is he a car salesman, or does he do something specialized?"

"Not sure," Link admitted, clicking through screens. "His title is Sales Manager, but he has partial degrees in business management and marketing." Frowning at the screen, Link muttered, "Wonder why he stopped going to college part-time."

"I'll find out," Rigel stated, trying to sound confident even though he was anything but. He reminded himself to have faith in the mate-pull and Fate's blessing. "And if he wants to do something other than sell cars, I'll support him in whatever he wants."

"We all will," Miggs claimed from where he sat on

Delanrue's lap, sharing the man's plate of food. The small man grinned at Rigel. "He's one of us now, even if he doesn't know it."

"Damn straight," Rigel agreed as the others grunted or muttered agreements.

Now if I can just convince him to give me the time of day, and if I can control my damn mouth and actions, I could move forward with my plan to woo my handsome Tucker.

The slip of paper in Rigel's pocket held his attention even as he listened to his buddies offer suggestions. He wasn't certain how long he would be able to hold out using it.

CHAPTER SEVEN

R igel had managed to give his mate three days. That was
plenty long enough to get over his anger with him, right?
He supposed it didn't really matter . . . not until he apolo-
gized again and reassured his mate that he would be there for
him.

To that end, instead of calling Tucker, Rigel decided to
show up at his door. Once Link had his mate's license plate
number, it had been easy for the tech-savvy man to get his
address. Between the tiny one-bedroom Tucker rented along
with the older, paid-for hatchback, Rigel wondered what
spawned him to live so frugally.

Just what does my mate spend his money on?

According to Link, Tucker didn't have a huge checking or
savings account balance. He had one credit card that he used
semi-regularly, probably just to keep it active. Tucker also
didn't have any pets or apparent hobbies. One odd thing Link
discovered was that every week, Tucker pulled five hundred
cash out of his checking account.

What the hell does Tucker spend that on?

Rigel hoped to find out.

To that end, Rigel prayed to whatever gods cared to listen
that Tucker wouldn't slam the door in his face. He gripped
the flowers he held in his left hand as he climbed the stairs to
the second-floor apartment. Rigel took a fortifying breath at
the door and found his senses assaulted with a fresh wash of
Tucker's scent, telling him he was home . . . or had been very
recently.

According to Link, Tucker had taken vacation that week.

Maybe he's trying to come to grips with what happened, or he's avoiding his father?

Considering Gary's homophobic hollering, Rigel wouldn't blame him. He hoped to convince his Tucker that he was better off without the bigoted human in his life. Rigel sure hoped his mate wasn't overly attached to his father because there was no way he wanted that sort of toxic attitude around Tucker on a regular basis.

Rigel finally gathered enough courage, lifted his hand, and lightly pressed the doorbell. Cocking his head, he listened to hear the tell-tale movements of someone within. It took a second ring of the bell, but Rigel finally heard it. Someone was shuffling toward the door.

When Tucker opened the door, it took every bit of self-control Rigel possessed not to allow his jaw to sag open, betraying his surprise. His mate looked rough. Tucker's hazel eyes appeared dim with sadness and uncertainty, his hair was unkempt, and his t-shirt was rumpled and had a coffee stain on it.

Even obviously in distress, Rigel thought Tucker was the most magnificent man in the world.

Tucker gaping at him drew Rigel's attention to his mate's mouth, but he figured capturing his lips first thing — again — wouldn't be his best move.

Use your words.

Recalling Dane, Del, and Link's repeated cautions, Rigel did just that. "Hi, Tucker." He forced his attention off Tucker's delectable mouth to look into his wide, hazel eyes. "I came to apologize." Rigel held up the bouquet of a dozen red roses. "Can I come in, please?"

Waiting for Tucker's response, Rigel just managed to keep from shifting from foot to foot like some untried youth.

I'm a nearly two-hundred-year-old shifter, damn it. I got this.

"H-How'd you find me?" Tucker asked after a few blinks,

as if coming out of his surprise. "What are you doing here?"

"Well, I'm here to apologize," Rigel repeated, jiggling the flowers just a little to draw attention to them. "And as for how I found you. Well, uh, I had a little help."

Tucker's eyes narrowed as he glanced from the flowers back to Rigel's face. "You followed me from the restaurant the other day, didn't you?" His voice lowered as he mumbled, "I thought someone was watching me."

Hmmm . . . good information, but —

"No, I didn't follow you," Rigel answered honestly. "May I come in?" When Tucker still didn't give him consent, he lowered his voice to a soothing rumble and tried, "I'm sorry I came on so strong. I just" — Rigel let out a deep sigh, trying to remember how his friends had encouraged him to start explaining things — "well, my family has this . . . belief . . . about being able to recognize that special someone who could be perfect for us right away." Doing his best to offer a depreciative chuckle, Rigel continued, "I've spent so many years alone that I began to think it was hooey. Then I met you and . . . handsome, you rocked my world."

"That's why you claimed I was yours?" Tucker slowly hazarded. "Because of some family . . . belief?"

Rigel nodded once. "Yes." He stretched out his arm with the flowers, trying again. "I know I came on a little strong. Can we talk about it?" When Tucker appeared doubtful, unease filling his scent, Rigel made a promise he sure as hell hoped he could keep. "I won't demand you're mine again . . . unless you're ready and you want it, too."

Tucker blew out a harsh breath. "You turned my orderly life upside down, Rigel," he snarled, his voice rising. Then, to Rigel's surprise, Tucker snapped out a hand and snatched the flowers. Turning away, he grumbled, "Get in here."

Okay. Not the best invitation, but I'll take it.

Following Tucker into his apartment, Rigel closed the door behind them. His senses were instantly inundated with the heavenly aroma of his mate. Rigel's cock thickened in his jeans so fast his head started to spin.

Rigel forced aside visions of Tucker sprawled out and writhing in his bed. He needed to focus on getting into his mate's good graces, and he didn't think pouncing on him would do it. Even though Rigel knew they would both enjoy it.

Focusing on his task wasn't easy when Rigel looked up and spotted Tucker's ass in his worn sweats. The faded gray fabric molded to his human perfectly. Rigel's hands twitched with his desire to cup those glorious globes.

Gods give me strength.

"You staring at my ass?" Tucker asked accusingly, peering over his shoulder at him.

Rigel knew he'd been caught. "Sorry, Tucker." With a shrug, he admitted, "I find everything about you . . . irresistible."

Tucker didn't look convinced, but he did turn his attention back to his kitchen. Opening the cupboard above the refrigerator, he pulled down a vase and filled it with water. After cutting the flowers' stems and adding the plant nutrient packet to the water, Tucker placed the flowers in the water.

Moving the vase to the kitchen island, Tucker focused on the flowers as he claimed, "Never gotten flowers from anyone before." A smile toyed around the corners of his lips. "It's, uh . . . sort of nice."

"Really?" Rigel moved to the other side of the counter, resting his hands on it. Considering how experienced Tucker had seemed getting the flowers set, if he hadn't had his nose to tell him that his mate was speaking truthfully, he would have been hard-pressed to believe him. "I know they're not traditional for a guy, but I wanted to bring something that would remind you of me after I left."

Tucker stared at the flowers for a moment, took a deep whiff of their scent, then straightened and met his gaze. "You want me to remember you?"

Rigel nodded once. As much as he wanted to round the island and gather Tucker into his arms, he knew that was his dick thinking. He wondered how long he'd been letting that particular part of his anatomy do the thinking because, damn, it was hard to resist.

Instead, Rigel rested his palms flat on the old Formica counter, rubbing his thumbs over the clean but aging plastic. "I wanted to apologize again for what happened in the restaurant." Feeling the heat rising up his neck, he didn't fight against it, allowing his mate to see his flush of embarrassment. "Your sister knew, so I just assumed your other family did, too." Rigel grimaced, knowing that wasn't an excuse. "And I probably shouldn't have grabbed you and kissed you the way I did, but I'll never apologize for kissing you. You taste too fantastic." Even knowing he was rambling, he couldn't quite make himself stop. "You'd snuck out that evening after an amazing night together. I thought you realized we were going to be more than a one-night stand, and finding you gone really threw me for a loop. I was already trying to find you, and then there you were . . . in the restaurant . . . and I — " Finally, Rigel managed to get his mouth to snap shut. His cheeks felt on fire, and he was having a hard time meeting Tucker's gaze, but he did it anyway because he knew he needed to know how his mate was taking his confession. Seeing Tucker's shocked look caused Rigel to wince. "Shit. Sorry."

"It's, uh — " Tucker paused and cleared his throat before starting again, his voice just as soft. "It's actually sort of nice to see you nervous, Rigel."

Hope filled him, and Rigel searched Tucker's face. "Yeah?"

"And now you sound like your over-confident self again," Tucker muttered with a sigh.

Shit. One step forward, two steps back.

"I don't mean to be," Rigel told him honestly. "It's just . . .

displaying confidence is important in my line of work."

"Oh, what do you do?"

Well, damn. That's a bit of a can of worms.

Keeping it simple, Rigel told him, "I'm in security at a private golf and spa resort just west outside of town." He hesitated again, trying to figure out how to bring up taking him on a date.

"Oh, you play golf?"

Rigel really didn't.

"Eh, not very good at it," Rigel replied evasively. Since it seemed to interest Tucker, he added, "But my gig does come with open passes to the course."

For just an instant, Rigel saw Tucker's expression brighten as he opened his mouth. Then he seemed to deflate as he looked away. His lips pinched together in a tight line.

So much for that idea.

Rigel decided to change tactics. "Look. I know you feel the chemistry between us." He knew from watching his friends' matings that their human partners felt the pull. "Please give us a chance. Let me take you to dinner tonight." When Tucker hesitated, Rigel pressed, "It's only four o'clock. I can come back in a couple of hours to pick you up. Have you eaten recently?"

Tucker glanced around the kitchen, which was clean, then down at himself . . . which was not. His cheeks darkened to a deep shade of pink. Looking to the left, Tucker grimaced as he rubbed a hand over the coffee stain as if trying to brush it away.

"Tucker, you're as handsome as always," Rigel claimed, hoping to ease his mate's sudden discomfort at realizing that he was a bit of a mess. "I know that you work for your father and that you took vacation time, probably to try to get your head wrapped around what happened." Needing to touch so badly, Rigel reached across the counter and rested his palm over Tucker's own. "I want you to know that you're not alone in this. I'll help in any way you want." He couldn't help but turn his voice entreating as he added, "Just please don't shut me out."

Seeing the struggle, the uncertainty, in Tucker's expressive hazel eyes, Rigel didn't know what else to say to convince him.

"Um, how'd you know I took vacation?" Tucker suddenly asked. "And you never explained how you found my home."

Happy to answer those sorts of questions, Rigel explained, "My buddy, Link, is a damn good tech guy." He shrugged as he admitted, "I'm not, so I don't know what sorts of programs he uses or what his processes are, but I gave him your phone number and license plate, and he pulled some background information on you so I could track you down . . . like your address."

Cocking his head, Tucker asked, "Where'd you get my phone number?"

"Your sister. Amelia." Rigel smiled faintly as he added, "She also made me promise I was serious about what could be between us. She didn't want me to unnecessarily cause havoc in your life if I wasn't going to stick around for the long haul." Cradling Tucker's fingers in his own, Rigel brought them to his mouth and pressed a kiss to his knuckles. He couldn't help the heat he knew infused his gaze as he stared at Tucker. "And, handsome, I'm in this for the long haul."

"But you don't know me." Tucker sounded confused as hell. "Why would you think that?"

"And we're back to my family's belief that we just . . . *know*." Rigel couldn't very well explain paranormals, shifters, and mates just yet. His mate needed more time. After landing another sipping kiss to his man's knuckles, Rigel persisted, "And dating fixes the problem of us not knowing each other."

"Dating?"

Rigel could smell Tucker's deepening arousal, and he was

beginning to struggle with his own needs. He'd been away from his mate for too damn long. If he didn't move things along and get out of there, Rigel was going to give in to his shifter instincts—and his dick—and see if he could find Tucker's bedroom . . . which wouldn't be all that hard in a one-bedroom apartment.

"Yes, Tucker," Rigel responded gruffly. "A date. This evening?" He stared into Tucker's slightly dilated eyes. "I know this wonderful Irish pub that serves delicious authentic fair. It's owned by my friend's husband." Rigel squeezed Tucker's hand once while rubbing his thumb over the pulse point of his wrist. "I can get us a secluded, romantic table, and no one will think twice about two men dining together."

Rigel mentally crossed his fingers, hoping Jin would be able to fulfill his request if Tucker accepted. From what fellow enforcer Tideus had told him, Wednesday could get a little busy. Maybe it was because it was the middle of the week, and business people were celebrating hump day.

Who knows.

"So, what do you say?" Rigel asked. "Can I come back at six-thirty and take you to dinner?"

With bated breath, Rigel waited . . . and waited.

Finally, just when Rigel began worrying he would have to do a little more convincing, Tucker gave one slow nod. "Okay."

Rigel couldn't help himself. As he murmured, "Thank you," he rushed around the counter, wrapped Tucker in his arms, and sealed his lips over Tucker's own. Just as before, his mate's flavor burst across his taste buds. Feeding his mate a moan, Rigel began to deepen the kiss.

Then Rigel caught himself and managed to rein it in before it got out of control. Breaking the kiss, he moved his hands to Tucker's trim waist and squeezed lightly. Smiling at the look on his mate's face, Rigel slowly released him and backed up a step.

"Later, Tucker," Rigel promised. "I look forward to seeing you soon."

Then Rigel fled before he gave in to his alligator's urging and took what they both desperately needed.

CHAPTER EIGHT

Maybe Tucker shouldn't have agreed, but he hadn't been able to help himself. Any time he was in Rigel's presence, he wanted to do nothing more than do whatever he needed to do to stay in the big handsome man's presence. Tucker didn't know if he could believe Rigel's claims about him believing they were special together—him being *the one*—Tucker couldn't resist finding out.

Well, that was how he felt when in Rigel's presence.

After Rigel had left, Tucker had begun to second-guess everything. True, the man had shown up with flowers and all the right words—and his kiss was electric—but was he really willing to turn his life upside down for him? Tucker was bisexual, after all. Couldn't he order Rigel to never contact him again? Then, if he didn't obey, he could get a restraining order.

That'd sure prove to my father I'm serious about . . . about . . . about being miserable and living a lie?

Shit!

Tucker knew that was the crux of the problem. Sure, he was bisexual and had enjoyed the attentions of women just as much as men, but he knew what Rigel was talking about. There really was something between them.

And if it hadn't been for Father, I'd be all over figuring out if what's between us could be long-term.

In all Tucker's years, he'd never considered an actual relationship with a man before. He'd had two long-term relationships with girlfriends, but only one-night stands with guys.

Tucker could admit, at least to himself, that it was because of his father's bigotry.

Just never wanted to create waves. I'm already in hot water with him. Maybe now's the time for change.

Except, what the hell will I do for a job then? How will I help out Amelia?

Tucker knew it wasn't just his own future on the line.

Not anymore.

His doorbell ringing pulled Tucker out of his unproductive thoughts. It was too late to cancel anyway.

And I don't even have Rigel's number if I did have time to cancel.

Shaking his head at his oversight, Tucker headed to the door. He still couldn't believe that Rigel had shown up at his door and called him handsome while he'd been in two-day-old and stained clothing. The man really had to be nuts.

Or really into me.

Tucker stopped before the closed door and rubbed the back of his neck. He knew opening the door could change his life. Was he ready for that?

The doorbell rang again . . . and Tucker just stood there.

"Tucker?" Rigel's deep voice came through the door. "I know you're there, handsome." Tapping lightly, he urged, "Please open the door, baby. Let me help ease your fears."

Unable to deny Rigel's soft crooning tones, Tucker opened the door. He felt his breath leave his lungs as he took in the man standing before him. The man had swept his dark hair away from his face, tying it behind him and showing off his bronzed, aristocratic features. The polo shirt molded to his wide shoulders and defined pectorals. Even the jeans seemed to draw attention to his thickly muscled legs without appearing to be obscene.

"Damn," Tucker whispered, shaking his head in awe. "You're stunning."

Rigel smiled as he eased forward, using a finger beneath Tucker's chin to get him to meet the man's deep brown eyes.

"Thank you, baby," Rigel rumbled, his pleased tone sinfully delicious. "You look fantastic, too." Then he dipped his head, but instead of kissing him, he angled for Tucker's neck. After a deep inhale, Rigel let out a husky groan. "Always smell so good. Can't get enough of you."

"B-But I'm not wearing any cologne," Tucker admitted. He'd thought about it, but he hadn't been able to make up his mind, so he'd skipped it.

"Love your natural scent, my mate," Rigel told him roughly, touching his nose to Tucker's neck and skimming it up and down the tendon. "So mouthwateringly delicious."

Then Rigel used a finger to ease the neckline of Tucker's polo a little to the side. His lips landed on the bite mark that still hadn't healed from Tucker's neck. The heated zings and tingles went straight to Tucker's groin, and he gasped as his cock thickened in his jeans.

"Fuck," Rigel whined, drawing away after bussing a kiss to his temple. "I'm sorry. Shit. So sorry." He moved his hands to Tucker's hips and shook his head as if trying to clear his own arousal. "Damn it. I need to be good." Then Rigel released him and took a step backward. "You're so much temptation, Tucker." Holding out a hand, palm up, he stated, "We should get out of here before I lose control of myself."

Even though Tucker knew he would enjoy Rigel taking him to bed, he knew that wouldn't solve their problems. The bedroom didn't seem to be a problem for them. Tucker needed to know if they had anything in common outside the bedroom.

Can't fuck all the time.

Except, as Tucker grabbed his keys from the nearby rack and took Rigel's hand, he knew that, with Rigel, it would be damn fun trying.

Gee-zus. Focus. Date first.

"Good thing I got us a secluded table," Rigel claimed as he

watched Tucker close and lock his door. "We're having trouble keeping our hands off of each other." Then, as he guided him to his vehicle, Rigel admitted, "But even there, two people going at it would be frowned upon. I'm sorry I'm having such trouble with my self-control." Grimacing, he assured, "I'll do better, handsome."

Tucker winced, admitting, "You're not alone."

And why is that? Why does this guy affect me so intensely?

"I'm so happy to hear that, Tucker," Rigel told him, guiding him down the stairs and to his SUV. His smile appeared tight as he opened the passenger door and stood beside it, obviously waiting for Tucker to climb inside. "Even though I know it makes us both damn uncomfortable at times."

Once Tucker was settled in his seat, Rigel reached for the belt as if he were going to buckle him in. "Uh, I get the door opening because you're just being polite," he began, holding up his hand to stay the big man's actions and draw his attention. "But buckling my belt is going a little too far."

Tucker had his pride and independence, after all.

Rigel froze, roving his gaze over Tucker's face. He offered a soft chuckle as he drew back, lifting his hands in placation. "Sorry about that." With a shrug, Rigel claimed, "Instinct to care for you."

Before Tucker could question that, Rigel shut the door. Watching him round the front, Tucker wondered what that meant. If Rigel was willing to buckle his seatbelt, just how far would he go to care for him? What all would that entail?

As Rigel climbed in behind the wheel, Tucker wondered how to phrase those questions.

Rigel started them moving, then reached over and rested his hand on Tucker's thigh. "I can practically hear the gears turning in your head, handsome." After a glance toward Tucker, Rigel refocused on making a turn. "Ask anything. I'll try to answer honestly."

"*Try* to answer honestly?" Tucker arched one brow while

doing his best to ignore the way the hairs on his leg stood on end just from having Rigel's palm resting there. "Um, shouldn't you say that you *will* answer honestly?"

With a shrug, Rigel admitted, "There are things about my family line that I can't share with you, yet, Tucker." He squeezed Tucker's thigh before moving his hand back to the wheel. "Differences, like how I realized you were the special *one* for me."

"And you can't tell me what they are?" Tucker wasn't certain how he felt about that. *What kinds of differences?* "You're not serial killers or something, right?"

Rigel barked a laugh as he shook his head. "Nope. Not serial killers." Grinning, he glanced Tucker's way again, his dark eyes twinkling with mirth. "And I'll tell you everything eventually. Once we get to know each other better." Rigel sobered as he admitted, "And I hope it doesn't take too long for you to accept our connection. Once you do, the . . . intensity of our attraction will temper a bit. Or so I've been told." Scoffing, he claimed, "Although I'll still want to jump your bones constantly. That's just the nature of our connection."

"Huh." Tucker didn't really know what to say to that. Curious, he asked, "So you've never felt this, um" — he waved his hand absently, searching for the right word — "this *pull* we feel toward each other?"

"Pull is the perfect word. Mate-pull." Rigel flashed another rakish grin his way. "And no, I've never felt this way toward another either." Furrowing his brows, he hurried to say, "Don't get me wrong. I like sex. Always have, and my friends will be the first to tease about me settling down, but I know you're it for me, Tucker."

Tucker felt his heart trip in his chest even as nerves fired through him. From Rigel's words, he could see that the other man already considered them a done deal. While Tucker could admit that their attraction was intense, he couldn't imagine being that certain of someone so swiftly.

No matter how much I'm attracted to him.

Wait.

"Did you say you've never been in a relationship?"

"Nope," Rigel confirmed. "Never have." As he spoke, he parked in a space on the side of the road. "So, please bear with me. I'm bound to make mistakes." Turning to focus on Tucker, Rigel murmured, "Like me claiming you're mine. I didn't mean to sound like a possessive asshole, but . . . well—" Rigel paused, his jaw flexing as if he struggled with how to finish. Tucker waited him out, curious, and Rigel finally stated, "I do consider you mine. Just like I consider myself yours."

"You're mine?" Tucker hadn't thought about it that way.

Rigel nodded once. "Yes, Tucker." Reaching over, he traced the backs of his forefingers along Tucker's jawline. "I'm totally and completely yours."

Tucker didn't know how to respond to that, especially with the way the hairs on his neck stood on end from Rigel's touch. The man certainly seemed touchy-feely, touching and caressing at every opportunity. Then it hit Tucker.

He's getting me used to his touch. Kinda like a person would a stray, semi-feral animal. Is that how he sees me?

Considering the way he'd fled after the one-night stand, then again in the restaurant, Tucker could see how Rigel might get that impression.

"Let's go eat, Tucker," Rigel urged, drawing away.

Relieved to take the reprieve, Tucker pushed open his door and climbed from the truck. He stood on the sidewalk, looking around the area. It wasn't a part of town he was familiar with and had a historical feel to it with plenty of brick buildings and wrought-iron light posts. He saw several restaurants and boutiques, and he wondered where they were going.

"Come on." Rigel arrived at his side and took Tucker's

hand, threading their fingers together. "This way."

Tucker almost pulled away, having never held hands with a guy before. Just like kissing, one-night stands didn't require or expect it. He resisted, reminding himself that Rigel was hoping for — or expecting — more.

Can I give it to him?

Tucker was still uncertain, even though he sure liked the idea of Rigel being all his. Could he trust it?

Rigel opened the door and guided Tucker inside, moving his hand to his lower back. The hostess greeted him with a smile. "Good evening, Rigel. Back already?"

Evidently, Rigel was a regular there.

"Hi, Sheila," Rigel greeted. "You know I can't ever get enough of Jin's cooking."

Then Tucker recalled Rigel telling him that the owner was the husband of one of his friends.

"I have a reservation for two," Rigel continued, sliding his arm around Tucker's waist. "First date."

"Oh, wow. Nice." Sheila grinned at Tucker for a few seconds before checking something on her podium. "Yep. Jin has set you up with a nice semi-secluded table in the back." She picked up a pair of menus and beckoned. "This way."

Tucker followed, feeling the weight of Rigel's arm around his waist the whole way. The hairs on the back of his neck stood on end, and he knew it was from nerves. Even though it didn't appear that any of the other patrons were paying them any attention, Tucker had never openly dated a guy before, and he was already in a precarious situation with . . . his life in general.

What the hell am I doing?

"Here you are, guys." Sheila showed them to a square table with four chairs. Instead of placing the menus opposite each other, she placed them before two chairs kitty-corner to each other. With a wide smile, she turned to face them. "Stacey will be your server this evening. Enjoy your meal."

Then Sheila headed back to the front, and Rigel urged Tucker toward one of the chairs.

"I can sense your nerves, Tucker," Rigel murmured once they'd both been seated. Reaching over, he placed his right hand over Tucker's left. "Are you willing to tell me what's wrong?"

Tucker almost flipped his hand over and gripped Rigel's as if it were a lifeline. Instead, he clenched his fist beneath the bigger man's warm palm. Frowning at the menu, not really seeing the words, Tucker tried to find a way to express his thoughts.

Except, they were a jumbled mess. He knew he wanted the man sitting next to him. He'd enjoyed their night together, and every time they were together, the magnetism was off the charts. While he wouldn't really call Rigel a gentleman, the man was straightforward and unapologetically into him.

But would he walk away when he realizes the burden I've taken on?

Tucker opened his mouth, ready to blurt out his troubles. "I—"

Then the waitress walked up and placed a pair of water glasses before them. "Hi, gentlemen. I'm Stacey, and I'll be your server this evening." She glanced between them, seeming to be oblivious to the fact that she'd just saved Tucker from possibly embarrassing himself and driving Rigel away. "Can I interest you in something more to drink than water?"

That was close.

CHAPTER NINE

Rigel wanted to throttle Stacey. He felt certain that Tucker had been about to share something important with him. The server's timing was absolutely abysmal.

But, since Rigel knew she was just doing her job, he forced a small smile to his lips and turned his attention to her. "Just a second." Rigel squeezed Tucker's fisted hand. "Do you like wine?" There were still so many things to learn about each other.

Tucker nodded. "White, not red." Cocking his head, he asked, "Is that okay? Or isn't it a man's drink?"

Scoffing, Rigel muttered, "I bet I know where you heard that." Then he pointed at a Riesling on the menu. "A bottle of that, please."

Stacey nodded, still smiling. She began to turn away, then hesitated and looked at Tucker. "Um, I'm afraid I'm going to have to see some ID, please."

Rigel relaxed back in his seat when Tucker pulled away so he could get out his wallet. His lover slid out his driver's license and handed it to Stacey. She looked it over for a moment before smiling and handing it back.

"Happy belated birthday, Tucker," Stacey told him. "With it being within a week, there's a free piece of Irish whiskey cake available to you, so save room."

"Oh, thank you," Tucker replied, returning his license to his wallet.

After Stacey left, promising the wine in short order, Rigel focused on Tucker again. "Your birthday? How old?"

"I turned twenty-six on Thursday," Tucker told him, taking a sip of water.

"The night we met," Rigel mused. Smiling, he waggled his eyebrows at him. "That'll make our anniversary easy to remember."

Tucker arched a brow. "Our anniversary?"

Rigel grinned. "Yep. Of the night we met."

"Uhhh, okay." Tucker cleared his throat and focused on the menu. In an offhand tone, he asked, "So, how old are you?"

Well, that's a can of worms.

It was Rigel's turn to clear his throat. "Uh . . . a lot older than I look," he muttered.

Tucker snapped his head up, giving him a questioning look.

That time, Rigel was grateful for Stacey's timely interruption. "Here's your wine, gentlemen," she stated, placing the glasses on the table. The top happened to be a twist-off so it was easy for her to open it. After pouring, she asked, "Which of you would like to sample it?"

Rigel indicated Tucker. "Give it a shot."

Tucker gave him a look like he knew he was avoiding, but his mate still took the offered glass. After taking a sip, he hummed and nodded before taking a larger swallow. He smiled and set the glass back on the table.

Stacey grinned and filled both glasses, leaving the bottle on the table. "Have you had a chance to decide on your appetizers?" she asked, holding up a small electronic tablet.

Considering Rigel had been there so often that he pretty much had the menu memorized, he hadn't bothered to look at it. He also knew what he wanted. Jin's shepherd's pie was one of his favorites.

"Did you have a chance to decide?" Rigel asked Tucker. "Or do you still need a minute?"

"Uh, I need a minute," Tucker admitted.

Stacey nodded and took a step backward.

"How about an order of your boxty appetizer to get us started?" Rigel requested. "And your assorted pasties."

With a smile, Stacey nodded again, quickly placing the order. "Perfect. I'll get those started for you." Then she headed off, promising to check in with them later.

Tucker chuckled. "I have no idea what you just ordered."

Grinning, Rigel flipped his own menu to the appetizer section and pointed at the items. "Boxtys are Irish potato cakes, and pasties are mini pies filled with either ground pork or beef and potatoes. The assorted order comes with both."

"Sounds good." Tucker hummed, turning his attention back to his menu. "I'm always up for trying something new. How are their bangers and mash?"

"You can't go wrong with them," Rigel assured. "Truthfully, everything Jin makes is fantastic."

"Nice. Like this place a lot, do you?" Tucker asked, closing his menu and refocusing on him. His eyes narrowed. "And don't think I didn't notice you dodged my age question. What's up with that?"

Rigel heaved a sigh and rubbed the back of his neck. "It's not that I don't want to tell you," he began slowly. "It's just one of those family things that I can't tell you about, yet." Grimacing, Rigel murmured, "Because I don't think you'll believe me, and you'll think I'm crazy."

"Kinda like you thinking you can find your forever partner just by looking at him?" Tucker's disbelief filled his tone.

"Yes," Rigel answered firmly.

"And that's why you've never been in a relationship?"

Rigel thought Tucker's guess was spot on. "Exactly," he confirmed. "What's the point of starting a relationship with someone when you know they're not your soul mate." Seeing Tucker's brows shoot up and his eyes widen, Rigel figured he'd said a bit much. That didn't stop him from resting his hand back over Tucker's and saying, "If I was in a relationship with someone else when I met you, I'd have hurt whoever that person was when I left them for you." Shaking his head, Rigel stated, "That wouldn't be fair to anyone."

"I guess I can see that," Tucker mused slowly. Then he quickly added, "If you believe in that sort of thing."

"Sort of thing?" Rigel pressed.

Tucker shrugged, but he didn't pull away from Rigel. "Yeah. The recognizing your soul mate as soon as you meet them thing."

Right. He doesn't believe me, yet.

Give it time.

"Ah," Rigel murmured, nodding slowly. He knew he would have to show Tucker his alligator to get him to believe him. Except, he had no idea when he should do that. How soon was too soon? "Well, I guess I'll just have to take it one day at a time to convince you that I'm the man for you."

"My soul mate?" Tucker smirked.

Rigel nodded slowly, pinning his mate with a serious look. "Yes, Tucker. We are soul mates."

Tucker arched a brow, still not looking convinced. "So lay it on me, then. Give me some clue on how you believe these things." Then Tucker gave him a challenging look. "If we're soul mates, then telling me something as simple as your age shouldn't be that big a deal."

"If you want the truth, I'll tell you," Rigel murmured, keeping his voice low so it couldn't carry to the next table. "But are you prepared to hear the truth?"

Licking his lips, Tucker appeared to be searching Rigel's face. He seemed to be searching for something, but Rigel wasn't certain what. Rigel continued to hold Tucker's gaze, hoping his mate found whatever he was looking for.

"Yeah, I want the truth," Tucker claimed quietly. "You already turned my life upside down once. What's another revelation?"

"Not everything in this world is as it seems, Tucker," Rigel told him softly, rubbing the back of his human's hand with his thumb. Then, taking a leap of faith, he told him, "I'm one hundred ninety-three years old."

Tucker's jaw sagged open, and his eyes widened. If the situation hadn't been so important, it would have been comical. The scent of disbelief quickly perfumed the air.

Rigel sighed. "You asked."

"How is that possible?" Tucker whispered, appearing to search his features again. Then he shook his head. "That's not possible."

"I told you that you wouldn't believe me, my mate." Rigel reached for his wine as he rolled his shoulder in a half-shrug. "I can give more explanations, but not here." He used his wine glass to indicate the rest of the restaurant. "This is not the place to discuss what most people would consider the paranormal."

"Paranormal?" Tucker murmured, his eyes narrowing. His hazel eyes took on a speculative gleam that Rigel wanted to question.

For good or ill, Stacey showed up once more. After taking their orders, she headed off again with the promise of returning in a couple of moments with their appetizers.

Blowing out a breath, Rigel refocused on Tucker. "Look. I know you don't believe me, and you have all kinds of questions." He glanced around quickly, then leaned closer to his mate and murmured, "And I want to answer them, but this isn't the place." After reiterating that warning, Rigel told him, "Just know that my age and my complete belief that we are soul mates are tied together."

Tucker stared him in the eye for several long seconds, making Rigel fight a case of nerves. Finally, he jerked a nod. "Okay." Reaching for his wine, Tucker murmured, "Everyone has secrets." He stared into his wine and asked, "So, what do you do for fun, Rigel?"

While Rigel knew they needed to change the subject, the abruptness unnerved him. He didn't like their serious subject's dismissal. Rigel would much rather have come to an agreement to discuss it later . . . preferably after dinner, at his house, and in his bed.

Except, I'm trying to give him time and be a gentleman.

Being a gentleman sucks, and not in a good way.

Wanting to please his mate, Rigel rolled with it. "I enjoy barbequing with friends, swimming, and hiking." He'd have to share at some point that most of the swimming he did was in alligator form. "I know you didn't see it the other night, but I have a greenhouse behind my place, and I enjoy growing my own vegetables and herbs."

"Wow, really?" Tucker sounded surprised, and Rigel smirked as he nodded. "I wouldn't have expected that."

Rigel chuckled, then told him, "After riding Dane's hog last week, I'm thinking about getting a motorcycle again." Arching a brow, he asked, "Did you enjoy riding with me?" When Tucker hesitated in answering, Rigel decided to goad him a little. "Maybe you'd like to drive your own? I can teach you. We can go on day trips to see the sights. I know the Drudeson brothers love to do that with their mates."

Tucker's eyes narrowed just a little, probably at Rigel's slip, but he didn't try to correct himself. Instead, he waited to see how his human would respond. Would he focus on the motorcycle comment or the reference to other men being mates?

"I don't think I'm going to have much time for those kinds of activities in a few months, Rigel," Tucker stated, surprising Rigel at how serious he sounded. "Look, even if I hadn't met you, my life would have changed soon anyway."

Squeezing Tucker's hand, Rigel asked, "Will you tell me what that means?"

Rigel had often heard that Fate brought mates together in their time of need. That could be why he'd run across Tucker at this time . . . to help his mate. Regardless of the reason or problem, Rigel was happy to have the human in his life.

Tucker nibbled his bottom lip for a few seconds, clearly debating. He opened his mouth, then closed it again. Using his chin to indicate to Rigel's left, Tucker smirked.

Following Tucker's indication, Rigel spotted Stacey bringing their appetizers. He chuckled, smiling at Tucker. The server really had the most bizarre timing.

After Stacey had dropped off the appetizers and confirmed whether or not they needed anything else, she headed off again.

As Rigel began placing several of each item onto a small plate for Tucker, he asked, "So, what were you going to say, Tucker?" He arched a brow. "What's changing in your life?"

When Tucker took the second plate, probably intending to get his own food, Rigel took it from him. He saw his mate's confusion in his eyes and smiled. As he placed the full plate before his human, he hoped his mate saw the action as caring for him and not crossing a line.

Like the seatbelt.

Hmmm . . . I may need to start asking.

Fortunately, Tucker didn't comment on the move. Instead, he picked up his plate and blurted out, "Amelia is pregnant. I'm going to help her raise the baby."

Rigel froze where he was filling the second plate for himself. The pastie he'd been holding slipped from his fork. His heart sped up in his chest.

That hadn't been what he was expecting . . . at all.

A baby.

Adding a few more items to his plate, Rigel processed that. If Tucker was going to be raising a baby, Rigel would be right there with him. Except, raising a human babe as a shifter wasn't an easy thing to do. Rigel would need to remake his identity at some point—Tucker's too—so that meant Amelia would probably have to be brought into the know at some point.

Would the kid need to be let in on the secret, too? Otherwise, we'd have to fake our deaths to our twenty-something son or daughter.

"Look. I know raising a kid isn't something you're probably wanting to sign up for, Rigel." Tucker's soft voice cut into Rigel's musings. "So we should probably stop this before we go any further."

"Oh, hell no," Rigel growled, frowning at Tucker. "I'm not walking away because of a baby. You're mine, and I'm yours." He winced at what he said, realizing he was once again being a possessive asshole. Still, Rigel couldn't help himself, continuing with, "That means if you're helping Amelia raise the baby, then I will, too. She's your family, so she's mine, too. That's the way it works." Curling his lip, Rigel muttered, "Of course, I'd rather not count your father as family, but you can't pick your in-laws, I guess."

By the time Rigel finished speaking, Tucker was gaping at him. His eyes were huge, and the scent of shock rolled thickly from him. Reaching over, Rigel gently closed Tucker's mouth with a crooked forefinger.

"I probably put my foot in it, didn't I?" Rigel began, realizing all the things he'd just blurted out. "But I'm not walking away because of a baby. I was just thinking logistics."

"Logistics?" Tucker shook his head as he stared at him with disbelief in his pretty hazel eyes. "Why would you want to saddle yourself with this mess?" Scoffing, he muttered, "As soon as my parents find out, my father will demand Amelia put it up for adoption or abort it, but my sister doesn't want to do either. She wants to keep it." Tucker frowned as he muttered, "Even if it turns out to —" Cutting himself off, he shook his head again.

"Turns out to what?" Rigel prodded, needing any and all information to help his mate.

Tucker flushed a little as he said, "Turns out to make our lives incredibly difficult."

"Why would caring for a baby make life difficult?" Rigel

didn't get it. "It's done every day by millions of people around the world."

Scoffing, Tucker told him, "My father is a domineering, overbearing man. If Amelia doesn't do as ordered, she'll be fired and cut off." He grimaced as he added, "You saw how he behaved in the restaurant. If I stay with you, he'll follow through on his threat. We'll both lose our jobs, and most of our friends are more hard up than we are and can't help us." Shaking his head, Tucker admitted, "Father says the dealership is a family business, so we don't make as much as normal employees. Instead, he keeps back about a third to reinvest in the company, and we're supposed to be like shareholders. But when he cuts us off, we'll lose that, too." Rigel could scent Tucker's agitation rising as he rubbed the back of his neck and continued, "I've been giving money to Amelia every week for doctor's visits and to start saving for when the baby's here. They're expensive. We plan to find a little two-bedroom to share while we figure out our next move and new jobs and—"

"Stop right there," Rigel ordered. Lifting Tucker's hand to his lips, he pressed a kiss to his knuckles. *At least that explains my mate's frugal nature and the weekly five hundred cash pulls.* "You are no longer alone, Tucker. I'm here, and I *will* help." Still seeing the disbelief in his mate's eyes, Rigel smiled warmly at him. "You'll see. Have a little faith." Then he waggled his brows as he added, "And I'm rich, so if you and Amelia didn't want to work another day in your lives, you wouldn't have to. You could stay at home with the baby, if you want." Using his words to gently remind Tucker that not everything about him was what it seemed, Rigel told him, "If you're good with money, nearly two hundred years is a long time to accumulate a fortune . . . and I'm damn good with money."

In a shocked whisper, Tucker murmured, "You'd really support all of us?"

Rigel knew he had so much to explain as he told his mate, "It's what someone like me does for their soul mate, Tucker." Knowing Tucker needed time to process his declarations, he pointed at the food. "Eat up, my mate. We'll discuss everything later."

To Rigel's relief, Tucker began to eat.

Damn. A baby. I have some phone calls to make.

CHAPTER TEN

The rest of the date rolled by in a whirl of great food, a little too much wine, and much lighter conversation.

On the drive home, Tucker was still trying to process everything that Rigel had claimed. The man actually expected him to believe that he would turn his life upside down by helping him, by helping his sister and a baby that wasn't his. Tucker had never heard of anyone doing any such thing for another.

Tucker didn't know if he could trust it.

Upon arriving home, Rigel walked Tucker to the door. After Tucker unlocked it and stepped inside, he noticed Rigel hadn't joined him. He turned and arched a brow questioningly.

"I've dumped a lot of information on you, Tucker," Rigel told him, answering his silent question. "I didn't know if you needed time to think about it, to process, I guess." Then his gaze heated as he raked it over Tucker. "And if I come in there, I won't be leaving until tomorrow."

Swallowing hard, Tucker felt heat flush his body. There was no mistaking that look. Arousal surged through him in response, and he clenched his ass even as indecision filled him.

Did he want Rigel to fuck him again?

Hell, yeah, he did. Except, that would clearly be sending the man the wrong message, right? If he let Rigel in, would his date think he was accepting everything he was saying—offering?

Do I want to accept that?
If it's true. Absolutely.

Unfortunately, Rigel was right. Tucker did need time to process. He needed to go over everything Rigel had said and done, trying to reconcile it in his mind.

"As much as I want to ask you in, I don't think I should," Tucker finally responded. He saw the flash of disappointment in Rigel's dark eyes and wanted to say — *fuck it* — and drag him inside. Tucker held fast, however, adding, "We've shared a lot of interesting things this evening, and I need to think about that." Resting his hand on Rigel's wide chest, Tucker felt the hard muscle there. His palm warmed, and the hairs on his arm stood on end. "But you're right. I need to think. Everything that's happened recently. It's — "

Tucker didn't know how to finish that — crazy, mind-numbing, insane, life-altering? They would all apply.

"I understand, Tucker," Rigel rumbled with a smile. Reaching out, he rested his hands on Tucker's hips. "This is a big step for you." His deep brown eyes narrowed as he pinned him with a gaze that could only be called feral. "I'll do my best to give you time, but I'm not going anywhere." Lowering his head, Rigel nuzzled Tucker's temple. "I'll help in small ways until you're ready to accept."

With that vow, Rigel sealed his lips over Tucker's. He suckled his lower lip, then nipped it. Pushing his tongue into his mouth, Rigel lavished him with a slow, languid kiss — so different than his prior ones — that set Tucker's blood on fire.

By the time Rigel brought the kiss to an end, Tucker nearly vibrated with need. His nipples were beaded, and his cock was hard as nails. Even his balls felt heavy, threatening to expel his seed with the slightest of touches.

"That's so you remember what you mean to me, Tucker, my mate," Rigel told him in a deep rough voice that betrayed his desire. "Your happiness, health, and pleasure mean everything to me, so I'll go now, but I'll be back." Dipping his head again, Rigel whispered into Tucker's ear, "I saw your golf clubs sitting in the corner of your living room." He nipped Tucker's lobe, causing the hairs on his nape to stand on end. "I'll pick you up tomorrow afternoon at two. We'll go play a round at the resort I work at."

Finally, Rigel lifted his head and smiled hungrily at him. "Be ready." Then he began easing away.

Tucker couldn't help his whine of dismay. His body nearly vibrated with need, and his lover was about to walk away.

Shit. I think of him as my lover?

"Oh, baby." Rigel moaned as he swept his gaze over Tucker. "I can't leave you like that." He glanced around, then stepped into the apartment and closed the door behind him. "Smelling of need and desire."

To Tucker's surprise, Rigel used his hold to spin him around. With his back to Rigel's chest, the bigger man urged him to lean against him. From the angle, Tucker realized the closed door supported their weight.

"Just relax and let go, my mate," Rigel crooned into his ear.

Then Rigel lowered his mouth to that sensitive spot on Tucker's neck . . . the mark Rigel had placed there . . . and licked it. A zing shot down Tucker's spine. Heat spread across his chest, causing his nipples to bead.

Unable to help himself, Tucker barked a cry of pleasure. He didn't know why Rigel touching there felt so good, he just knew it did. Then Rigel reached around and cupped Tucker's groin, massaging his cock through his jeans. At the same time, his lover sucked on his neck.

Crying Rigel's name, Tucker came. His body jerked as he unloaded in his jeans in hard, ecstasy-inducing spurts. His body sung with bliss as Rigel moaned against his flesh and continued to work his cloth-covered dick.

Finally, when Rigel lifted his mouth from Tucker's neck and moved his palm over his stomach soothingly, his senses began to settle. He panted harshly, trying to catch his breath.

Leaning heavily against the other man, Tucker blinked slowly, trying to get the room back into focus.

"I-I don't know how y-you do that to me," Tucker croaked, his voice shot from crying out his pleasure. "H-How?"

"We are soul mates, my love," Rigel crooned into his ear. "Our bodies long for each other, for us to couple and become one."

Tucker wasn't certain if he didn't understand that because his brain was still fuzzy from his release or if it was another one of Rigel's odd beliefs. Still, he could so get used to Rigel's sweet, drugging kisses. Not to mention, the guy's hands and mouth were magick.

"You feeling better now, Tucker?" Rigel asked, pecking a kiss to his temple.

Snickering, Tucker mumbled, "Better than better." Registering the dampness of his crotch, he winced. Then he realized Rigel had gotten him off, but he hadn't done anything for the other man. Peering over his shoulder, Tucker rocked his hips back as he offered, "Can I return the favor?"

Rigel gave him a feral smile as he told him, "No need." He paused and pecked a kiss to Tucker's lips. Lifting his head, Rigel admitted, "I came when you did."

"You did?" Tucker eased forward, getting his feet under him.

Rigel nodded. "Yep." His brown eyes appeared warm with satiation. "Watching you, feeling you come in my arms, smelling your seed." Rigel hummed in obvious appreciation. "Delicious. Sent me right over the edge."

"Oh, wow," Tucker whispered. No one had ever enjoyed pleasuring him so much that they got off on it. That was heady knowledge right there. Making a decision—maybe a bad one, since his brain was still a bit mushy—Tucker stated, "I look forward to seeing you tomorrow at two."

Rigel's beaming grin warmed Tucker, and he realized he

enjoyed pleasing the other man just as much.

After one more sweet kiss from Rigel, his lover promised, "See you tomorrow," before heading out the door.

Tucker watched him head down the stairs and climb into his truck. Shutting and locking the door, he couldn't help the happy smile curving his lips.

Tucker woke to the sound of someone pounding on his door. With a groan, he slipped from his bed. He grabbed a pair of sweats and a t-shirt before glancing at the clock.

Who would be visiting me at nearly nine in the morning on a Thursday?

A look through his peephole gave Tucker his answer. His father stood on the other side of the door. From the dark scowl and flushed face, he didn't look happy.

Maybe I can pretend I'm not home.

"Open the damn door before I use my key, Tucker." His father hollered the order.

Right. I gave Mom my spare key.

After letting out a heavy sigh, Tucker unlocked the door and opened it. He quickly took a step backward so his father didn't run him over when he barreled inside. Tucker debated leaving the door open but decided that would probably enrage his father further.

Tucker closed the door and followed his father into the small dining room. "Good morning, Father," he greeted, doing his best to sound calm. "Can I get you a cup of coffee?"

Moving past his father into the kitchen, Tucker proceeded to pull a couple of mugs from the cupboard. He turned to the brewed pot, appreciating the invention of timers. Tucker poured himself a cup, then turned his attention to his father, awaiting his answer.

The malice in Gary's eyes made Tucker's breath catch. He almost took an involuntary step backward. A fissure of unease trickled down his spine.

Tucker couldn't remember ever seeing his father so angry.

"No, I don't want a cup of coffee," Gary snarled. As Tucker placed the carafe back on the warmer, he watched his father stalk toward him. "You've had several days of vacation to get your head on straight." His father curled his lip as he lifted some papers he carried. "Instead, I find out you're cavorting with that faggot and flaunting your deviant ways."

Gary slapped some pictures on the kitchen counter, and they slid across the Formica, spreading out.

Looking over the pictures, Tucker felt his mouth go dry. They were pictures . . . of him and Rigel. They'd been on their date the night before.

The first showed them walking down the sidewalk outside the restaurant, hand in hand. One showed his lover leaning close to him at the table. Another showed Rigel standing in the doorway of Tucker's apartment, his arms braced on the molding as he peered at him, his expression one of clear desire. Finally, there was a picture of Rigel entering Tucker's apartment, the door half closed.

"What do you have to say for yourself?" his father yelled, causing Tucker to jump.

Hot coffee splashed over Tucker's hand, and he hissed. He quickly set his drink aside and grabbed a paper towel. Tucker's mind spun as he cleaned the mess. He even took a second to crouch on the floor to wipe up the coffee there, trying to buy time to think.

That was a mistake.

His father stepped forward and backhanded Tucker across the face, yelling, "Answer me."

Pain exploded across Tucker's cheek as he flopped backward onto his ass. He quickly scrambled back to his feet, moving around the island to get away from his father. Tucker's father had never struck him before, and his mind reeled in disbelief.

Rubbing his cheek, Tucker snapped, "What the fuck, Father?"

"If you're a fucking faggot, I'm not your father," Gary declared with a snarl. "It means you're just another abomination that needs to be taught a lesson." He pointed at the pictures again. "Are you seeing him again? Or did that hit make you come to your senses?"

Anger surged through Tucker, and he felt a muscle tick in his jaw. "I'm seeing Rigel again," he declared, choosing his ultimatum—for better or worse. "Today, in fact, since you forced vacation on me."

"Sure you don't want to rethink that, boy?" Gary growled, beginning to unbuckle his belt. "Maybe you just need a bigger lesson."

Tucker froze for an instant as shocked reality hit him. His father intended to beat him into submission.

Oh, hell, no.

Pulling his phone from the pocket of his sweats, Tucker woke it and dialed nine-one. Hovering his hand over the third digit, he snapped, "Just try it. Father or not, I'll be happy to press charges." Narrowing his eyes, Tucker watched his father hesitate. "I'm sure your friends at that damn country club you love so much would sure enjoy hearing about how you accosted your son in his own home."

Gary's face turned a dark purple hue, and his features twisted with rage. "You're fired," he rasped, buckling his belt again. "Don't bother coming in for your last check. It'll be mailed."

When Gary began stalking around the island, Tucker matched his father step for step, making certain to keep it between them. "You can't fire me for my sexual orientation," Tucker declared, not that he would want to keep working there anyway.

Sneering, Gary swept a disgusted gaze over him. "Don't worry, faggot. I'll think of something." His eyes narrowed as he added, "And never contact any of us again."

With that parting shot, Gary opened the door so hard it slammed into the backstop before stalking out of Tucker's apartment.

Tucker hurried forward and closed the door. After locking it, he rested his back against it and let out a long sigh.

Well, I made my choice, didn't I?

Lifting his phone, Tucker deleted the two digits he'd entered. Then he called Amelia.

"Hey, Tuck," Amelia greeted warmly, making Tucker smile. "How's your forced vacation going?"

"Interesting," Tucker answered. Then he shared parts of his date that didn't make Rigel seem insane, as well as their father's visit. Eventually, Tucker finished with, "It looks like we're going to have to move up our plans."

"I'll put in my notice today," Amelia told him, worry filling her voice. "We'll be okay. Won't we?"

Tucker thought of Rigel's offer and answered, "We'll be just fine."

CHAPTER ELEVEN

When Tucker opened the door, Rigel's smile slipped from his lips. His focus was riveted on the red, slightly swollen mark on the man's cheek. Someone had struck his mate.

Rigel lifted his hand to his mate's face, hating how Tucker flinched. "Easy, baby," he crooned, finishing the move and gently resting his palm below the mark. "Who did this? What happened?"

All sorts of ways to get revenge filled him.

"My father," Tucker revealed. Rigel couldn't bite back his growl, and his mate hurried to add, "But don't worry about it. His image is everything, and I threatened to press charges." Snorting, Tucker grumbled, "Not only is it not good for him to have a faggot son, but being charged with assault would be equally damning."

"A faggot son?" Rigel scowled, not pleased by the language. "Did you go see him or something?"

Why would his mate do that? Worry filled Rigel that he hadn't made as deep inroads into getting Tucker to accept him as he'd thought. What if he'd gone to see him to ask about his job or to deny him?

Tucker shook his head. Taking a step backward, he beckoned. "No. Someone followed us on our date." He pointed toward the kitchen. "My guess would be a PI, and they gave pictures of us together to Gary."

"Gary?" Rigel questioned as he crossed the room. He found it interesting that Tucker hadn't called the man his father.

Shrugging, Tucker stated, "He said I'm no longer his son and never to contact anyone again." He curled his lip and added, "I'm also fired, but don't come in to pick up my last check. It'll be mailed."

"Gods, I'm sorry, Tucker."

Guilt surged through Rigel. After all, he'd been the one to open that particular can of worms, even if by accident. Then Rigel spotted the photos and picked them up. They really were all fairly innocuous. Then Rigel spotted the one of him in the doorway staring at Tucker. Unable to help himself, he hummed with appreciation. While Rigel's own expression screamed desire, Tucker's answering look was just as heavy-lidded and hungry.

Yup. No mistaking that.

"Don't worry about it," Tucker offered softly, standing right beside him. For the first time in their relationship, his mate initiated touch, resting his hand on Rigel's back. "Like I told you before, I would have ended up needing to leave the company anyway." With a shrug, Tucker told him, "This just moved up our timeline. That's all." Then he grimaced and rubbed his cheek with his free hand. "Of course, I could have done without the slap, but he did that before I told him I planned to continue seeing you."

"Our timeline?" Rigel put the pictures down and turned, wrapping his arms loosely around Tucker's waist. He loved having his mate in his arms. His heart swelled with the knowledge that Tucker had chosen him over his bigoted, toxic father. "What do you mean?"

"Amelia is putting in her notice today." Tucker nibbled his bottom lip for a few seconds, and Rigel waited patiently. Meeting Rigel's gaze once more, he asked, "Were you serious about helping us?"

"Of course, my mate," Rigel confirmed, rubbing his thumb over Tucker's hip bone. "I'm here for you, your sister, and the babe." Enjoying Tucker's relieved expression, Rigel absently asked, "Does Amelia know who the father is?"

"Um, sort of." Tucker glanced away, shifting his weight from foot to foot, and discomfort filled his scent. "He was really a one-night stand's contraceptive mishap, but when she told him about being pregnant, he refused responsibility and scared the shit out of her." Grimacing, Tucker muttered, "Probably for the best. She read his name in an obituary. Died in some kind of warehouse fight between rival gangs." He blew out a breath as he shook his head. "Guess even bad guys can be charming at times because no way is my sister's judgment that bad."

Rigel nodded slowly, something niggling at him upon hearing that explanation, but he couldn't put his finger on it. "For the best then." He dismissed the issue, since the man was dead. With a wink, Rigel claimed, "We'll be much better fathers to the babe."

Tucker scoffed. "I hope so."

"Come on." Rigel pecked a kiss to Tucker's lips, just because he could, before urging his mate to turn. "Let's get going."

Rigel really wanted to get Tucker into shifter territory so he could find a way to start explaining things. "I'll grab your clubs if you want to snag your keys." It was time to move their relationship along.

An hour and a half later, Tucker laughed as Rigel managed to sink another ball into a water hazard.

Rigel groaned as he rolled his eyes. "I warned you."

"You did. You really aren't very good at golf." Tucker rested his hands on his hips and eyed him. His hazel eyes danced with mirth. "You sure you want to continue? Are you even enjoying yourself?" A bit of concern filled his scent. "I mean, I don't want you doing something you don't even like just for me."

Appreciating the sentiment, Rigel closed the distance between them. "Even though I suck at golf, I'm enjoying myself because I'm with you." He lowered his head and captured Tucker's lips in a deep short kiss. When he straightened, Rigel took in Tucker's pleased yet bemused expression. "Really," he assured. "Any time with you is enjoyable."

"You're a little sappy, Rigel," Tucker teased. Although his scent screamed his pleasure. "I wouldn't have expected that."

"Only sappy for you, my mate," Rigel claimed, okay with the assessment if it made Tucker happy. "I suppose I'll need another ball." With a wink, he eased away from his human as he told him, "There are groundskeepers who go swimming for them."

Rigel didn't tell Tucker that those people were aquatic shifters whose animals enjoyed the task. Even Rigel's alligator performed the duty on occasion. After all, he loved swimming, and he, Dakota, and Dane would make a competition of it.

Whoever retrieved the most golf balls got free beers from the others.

"Good thing you brought several boxes." Tucker grinned over his shoulder at him as he headed toward where they'd left their golf bags in the cart. "I thought it seemed like a lot, but now it makes sense."

Chuckling, Rigel appreciated that Tucker was willing to tease him.

"So." Tucker reached into Rigel's bag and retrieved a ball. "Are you ever going to explain why you call me your mate?" he asked, heading back toward him. "Wait. Didn't you say something about the Drudeson brothers having mates?" Tucker's eyes widened, and he paused halfway to him. "Does it mean that soul mate thing you talked about? Husband? Partner?"

"All of the above, Tucker," Rigel answered honestly,

pleased with the opening. He thought it was the perfect opportunity. "You see, when I told you I'm almost two hundred years old, I was telling you the truth. I can live that long because I'm something called a shifter. I can shift into an animal form. An alligator." Seeing the way Tucker's eyes widened and how he took a step backward, Rigel dropped his club and lifted both hands in placation. "Please, handsome. Even when I'm in alligator form, I'm completely cognizant. I know everyone around me and can still think and reason."

Maybe I should have eased into it a little bit better.

"A shifter?" Tucker whispered, sounding and scenting of shock. "An alligator?"

Rigel nodded, pleased that Tucker was at least asking questions and not running. "I share my psyche with a large American alligator, but I would never hurt you. You're my mate. The other half of my soul."

In for a penny, in for a pound.

"I told you I recognized you as my mate, that Fate brought us together." Rigel started forward, one slow step at a time. "Our souls and bodies cry out for each other, wanting to touch and bond." Recalling how soothing touch could be, Rigel hoped he could reach Tucker before his human took off. His mate looked tense enough to run, and he really didn't want to chase him down. "Once we bond, our insatiable need will ease a little, although we'll always still want each other."

Tucker stared at him with furrowed brows and an inscrutable expression, and Rigel took the opportunity to ease a little bit closer.

"I'm sure you have questions, Tucker," Rigel continued, hoping to keep his mate engaged. "I'll answer every single one. You're my mate, and I'm honored to have finally met you." With a soft laugh, Rigel admitted, "I've dreamed of meeting you more times than I could count, but nothing could have prepared me for the actual moment of first scenting you. Holding you in my arms. Of kissing you and loving on you."

Tucker opened his mouth, but the low hiss of an animal caused him to snap it shut again.

Jerking his attention to the reeds near the edge of the pond, Rigel frowned. He knew what it sounded like, but surely no shifter would be stupid enough to interrupt . . . especially not like that. Except, a second later, Rigel found himself proved wrong.

Lydia, in crocodile form, came easing from between the reeds. Focusing on Tucker, she hissed menacingly. She opened her jaws and growled, revealing row upon row of sharp, jagged teeth.

"Lydia, back off," Rigel ordered darkly, pushing authority into his voice. Glancing toward Tucker, he softened his tone when he assured, "It'll be fine, baby. Trust me."

Tucker looked from the crocodile to Rigel and back to the animal. "Y-You, uh, you sure?" he whispered, slowly backing a couple of steps.

Rigel noticed Tucker was retreating toward the golf cart as opposed to him. While he understood why his mate would do that, it also put more space between them. He didn't like that.

When Lydia let out another hissing growl and advanced another step toward Tucker, Rigel let out his own snarl of warning. "Back off, Lydia," he growled. "One more step toward my mate, and I will defend accordingly."

Opening her jaws wide, Lydia let out a roar. A second later, she charged toward Tucker.

While Rigel had no clue what had gotten into the damn shifter, he didn't give his actions another thought. He streaked toward Lydia's attacking crocodile, shifting as he went. As a council enforcer, Rigel had worked hard to perfect his shift. After three steps, he was on all fours. His body expanded swiftly, rending his clothes and littering the ground with fabric scraps.

Rigel reached Lydia just as she went to snap at a running Tucker's leg. Grabbing her tail in his jaws, Rigel jerked his head to the left, sending her sprawling. Lydia rolled, tumbling away from Tucker and toward the shore of the pond.

Swiftly, Rigel positioned himself between Lydia and Tucker. He watched her crocodile right herself and whip back around to face him. Lydia growled, her jaws parting. Rigel returned the aggressive snarl, watching her carefully.

While Rigel had no idea what the hell was going on with Lydia, he sure as shit wasn't letting her near his mate. Going after a mate was a death sentence, even an unbonded one, once the connection was declared. Lydia should have backed off.

However, Lydia didn't back off. She seemed to be considering her options, her attention moving from his defensive position to his mate beyond him. Lydia scuttled sideways a few steps, perhaps testing him.

Rigel countered, keeping himself between the slightly larger reptile and the golf cart. He figured he would hear the low whine of the cart's engine any second, but so far, it'd been quiet. While Rigel wondered what Tucker was doing, he wasn't about to take his attention off the crocodile to find out.

With a roar, Lydia attacked.

The sudden move surprised Rigel so much, he nearly didn't react in time. At the last second, he twisted left. Swinging his tail around, Rigel slammed it into Lydia's snout in a whip-like move.

Lydia skidded across the grass. Rigel took the opportunity and turned, hitting her front leg with his tail. When Lydia's front end went out from under her, Rigel charged.

Rigel reached Lydia just as she managed to get back to her feet. Sliding his snout under a foreleg—what would be the armpit of a human—he snapped his head upward. The force of the move caused Lydia's crocodile to flop onto her back.

Pouncing, Rigel wrapped his jaws around Lydia's neck. The crocodile tried to roll, but he sank his teeth into her hide in warning. Her blood welled up between his teeth, and she froze on her back.

Growling loudly, Rigel demanded her submission. It took a moment, as if Lydia was actually contemplating if she could get out of his hold, before she finally obeyed. Rigel didn't release her, however. Instead, he snarled again as he flexed his jaws just a little.

To a shifter, Rigel's meaning was clear.

Shift, or I'll kill you.

Lydia obeyed and shifted. After about ten seconds, when she appeared about halfway through her transition, Rigel released her and initiated his own shift. He completed his before Lydia had finished.

Rigel had intended to grab her and demand answers, but he didn't have to. Dane grabbed her as soon as she was human and hauled her to her feet. The fellow enforcer tugged Lydia's arms behind her back, cuffing the naked, fuming woman.

"Seems your mate knows about shifters, Rigel."

Dakota's amused voice caused Rigel to snap his attention toward the cart. Unable to help himself, he gaped at what he saw. While Tucker appeared pale, and he held the side of the cart in a white-knuckled grip, he hadn't run. In fact, he stood behind the cart and held a cell phone in his hand . . . one Rigel recognized as his own.

Delanrue rested a hip against the hood of the golf cart, and he had his arms over his chest. He sported a dark expression, and he eyed Lydia.

Dakota rested his forearms on the golf cart's frame where he stood next to Tucker.

"What the hell?" The words were out of Rigel's mouth before he could stop them. "You know about shifters?"

"I know *of* them," Tucker whispered, his voice barely carrying to Rigel. "Just that they exist. Although"—he glanced around at everyone—"I didn't know I'd met any until you started explaining... *things*." Tucker waved his hand in a circular motion. Pointing at Lydia without looking at her, his mate told him, "I figured since you talked about the Drudeson brothers and mates, they were like you, so I called them when, um... she attacked." Frowning, Tucker shook his head. "Why did she attack me?"

"Because Rigel is mine," Lydia screamed. "He's not supposed to take care of some stupid human. He's supposed to take care of me!" With a red face, she continued, "You were looking at *me* before this human came along. You want *me*!"

"I looked at everyone before Tucker came along," Rigel admitted, shaking his head. "Doesn't mean I would have ever done anything with you." Wincing, he jerked his attention back to Tucker. "I'm sorry. I warned you that my friends called me a player. But you're my mate, and I'll be completely faithful to you."

"No," Lydia screeched again. "You're mine."

"Take her away," Delanrue ordered his brother. "I've had enough of her stupidity."

As Dane shoved her across the lawn, Lydia bucked and tried to wriggle from his hold. The larger enforcer easily subdued her, pushing her forward.

"You're lucky, Lydia," Delanrue called. "If you'd gone after my mate, I would have ripped your throat out and asked questions later."

By that time, Dane had taken the extra step of gagging her, but that didn't stop them all from hearing her muffled slurs before she was out of earshot.

Rigel turned back to Tucker and slowly neared him. To his pleasure, his mate grabbed him in a hug while asking, "Are you all right?"

"I'm all right," Rigel assured, hugging his mate back. Kissing his human's temple, he couldn't help but ask, "How do you know of us?"

CHAPTER TWELVE

Tucker blew out a breath, knowing it was time to lay it all out there. "The asshole that knocked up Amelia, well" — he always hated thinking about his sister having sex — "well, he was a shifter."

The man who'd introduced himself as Delanrue arched one blond brow. "Why would Amelia know about shifters?" He scowled. "Was her baby-daddy her Fated mate?"

"Uh, no." From context, Tucker understood the difference between a Fate-given mate and one a shifter decided to choose. "They were a one-night stand," he muttered, glancing away. "But when Amelia realized she was pregnant, she tracked him down." Grimacing, Tucker tightened his hold on Rigel, taking comfort in the man's arms. "Some guy named Kennedy. Amelia said he turned into a rhinoceros and bluff-charged her until she left."

Rigel growled softly before pressing a kiss to the top of Tucker's head. "Kennedy was what law-abiding shifters call a rogue. He was part of a group that were breaking our laws." Shaking his head, he explained, "Keeping the secret about our ability to shift is rule number one in our community. Except for our Fated mate, we never purposefully tell anyone without our higher-ups' permission." Rigel winced as he told him, "If Kennedy wasn't already dead, he would have been in a shit-load of trouble for his actions, and Amelia would have been taken care of for life, with our community helping her raise her shifter child."

Tucker nodded slowly, glad to hear that shifters had some

sort of self-governing body to keep humans safe from them. "So, the child will definitely be a shifter?"

"He or she will. A shifter's DNA will always dominate over a human's," Dakota confirmed, offering him a reassuring smile. "Don't worry. You all will have plenty of support." He offered a roguish smile as he added, "Especially with Rigel being your mate and all." Reaching over, Dakota patted him lightly on the shoulder. "You're in good hands, man."

"Rigel, maybe you should take Tucker back to your suite and discuss bonding with him." A corner of Delanrue's lips curved into the faintest of smiles. "The pheromones you two are putting off are quite intense." The blond's cool hazel eyes swept down their bodies, pausing at their groins. "And it's not as if you're hiding anything, Rigel."

Frowning, Tucker eased a bit to the left, hiding Rigel's arousal from Delanrue's view. "Then don't look," he grumbled.

"Sorry, handsome," Rigel rumbled huskily. "I can't help it. Not until we've completed our bond." Then he scoffed as he added, "And probably not even then."

"How does one bond?" Tucker asked. A second later, he had to know something else. "Is bonding with a shifter like marriage?"

"For a Fated pair, bonding is entwining your life threads," Dakota stated from the back of the golf cart where he appeared to be looking for something. "Marriage without divorce, but the shifter is instinct-driven to please, pleasure, and keep safe his or her partner." Popping his head up, Dakota tossed a pair of sweatpants at Rigel. "There ya go, man." Then he grinned at Tucker, his green eyes twinkling. "And a bonded shifter can never cheat. Can't even get it up for another. And he'll never purposefully hurt his mate, by word or deed."

"Accidents do happen," Rigel cut in as he pulled on the

pants. Then he quickly took Tucker back into his arms. "But I'll do my best for that to never happen." Threading the fingers of one sun-bronzed hand through Tucker's hair, Rigel told him, "I want you safe and happy." Then he waggled his brows and growled, "Well-fucked, too, if you're amenable."

Heat rushed through Tucker's body upon hearing Rigel's words. The man's touch always ramped him up so fast. While Tucker was getting the idea that it was a shifter mate thing, he couldn't say that he minded. Before Rigel, Tucker'd had a hell of a dry spell, and after everything his lover had done to him that night, his body was damn near begging for a repeat.

"Yeah, it's time for you guys to go, Rigel," Delanrue drawled. "The rest of your explanations should be done in your room."

"Probably naked," Dakota piped up, laughing and grinning.

Rigel peered down at Tucker hungrily. "Is that okay with you, Tucker?"

Tucker appreciated that Rigel offered him the choice. However, to his mind, there wasn't any choice to be had. His body always seemed primed when around Rigel, and even after seeing him face off with another as an alligator, that hadn't changed. In fact, seeing his lover's prowess in battle had Tucker wanting him even more.

"Take me to your suite, Rigel," Tucker ordered.

Groaning, Rigel moved quickly. He urged Tucker onto the passenger seat. Then he bounded around to the driver's side. A second later, Rigel had them racing down the paved pathways through the golf course.

It didn't take long for the resort to come into view, and Tucker wondered where they were going.

"Uh, do you have a room here at the resort?" Tucker wondered, thinking maybe security guards might have somewhere to rest.

"A suite," Rigel told him. "This is much more than a golf resort and spa." With a glance Tucker's way, he explained, "This is actually Shifter Council Headquarters. The resort's a cover." Parking the golf cart near a back patio, Rigel urged Tucker out and began leading him between metal tables to a set of French doors. "I'm an enforcer for the council, guarding councilmen and helping bring rogues in for justice." Wrapping his arm around Tucker's waist, Rigel explained, "Each enforcer and councilman has a small suite of rooms here, just in case they need a place to change, clean up, or recharge between assignments, and there isn't enough time for them to go home."

A few minutes later, Tucker discovered that the words *small suite of rooms* was relative. He stepped through the door Rigel had unlocked using a code on a keypad and froze. The place looked like a large suite in a fancy hotel.

The small foyer gave way to a living room with comfortable sofas and chairs, a coffee table, and a couple of end tables. There was a large flatscreen on the wall, a gas fireplace beneath it, and a desk pushed against a wall off to the side. On the other side of the room was a small kitchenette with a mini fridge, microwave, and two-burner stove.

Through a couple of open doors, Tucker made out a bathroom, as well as a bedroom.

Rigel pointed toward the bathroom. "Need it before I lay you down and ravish you, my mate?"

Tucker felt a shiver of need work through him. His mostly hard prick thickened the rest of the way behind the fly of his jeans. Even his nipples beaded when he heard Rigel's blunt words in his deep voice laced with need.

"J-Just, um—" Tucker paused and cleared his throat. "Just assuming, huh?"

Groaning, Rigel pressed his back against the closed door. He lifted his hands and threaded them through his hair. He blew out a breath as he eyed Tucker with a gaze mixed with lust and resignation.

"I-I can wait." Rigel's voice sounded damn strained. Lowering his hand to his groin, he cupped himself as he muttered, "I'll just have to, uh, use a few minutes in the bathroom first to—"

"Don't you fucking dare," Tucker growled, lowering to his knees. He'd wanted to taste Rigel since that first day. No way was he going to miss the opportunity now. As Tucker pushed down Rigel's sweatpants, he declared, "This is mine."

At the appearance of Rigel's long, thick flesh, Tucker hummed appreciatively. He quickly opened his mouth and wrapped his lips around his lover's crown. He sucked strongly, enjoying the masculine, slightly salty flavor that burst across his tongue. Rigel tasted better than anything Tucker had enjoyed in longer than he could remember, and he sank deeper, hoping to draw out more pre-cum as he sucked up.

"Tucker," Rigel cried, a shudder rolling through his big body. "Fuuuuck," he snarled, his pleasure evident by the way he twitched in Tucker's mouth. Rigel threaded his fingers into Tucker's hair and cradled his head. "So hot. So perfect." Rigel began thrusting slowly, working his erection in and out of Tucker's mouth, and he did his best to suck and stimulate with each move. "Oh, yesssss, my mate. Just like that."

Knowing he couldn't take all of Rigel's long, thick prick, Tucker wrapped one hand around his lover's base, keeping him from going too deep. He gripped the bigger man's hip, steadying himself as Rigel picked up his thrusts. All the while, Tucker used his tongue to lap over his crown, tickle the sensitive flesh beneath the head, and trace along the swollen vein running along the underside.

"Close, my mate," Rigel warned, his voice husky and ragged. "So fuckin' close." Moaning deeply, he rumbled, "Gods, your mouth. Fuck!"

Even as Rigel's rhythm faltered, heralding his imminent release, he never pushed too hard or tried to get too deep. He respected Tucker's hand placement, its silent warning. Instead, Rigel hissed and shuddered and moaned his name.

"Mate!"

Rigel's hollered word was all the warning Tucker received before his mouth was filled with a thick spurt of cream. The heavy burst surprised him, and he jerked back a bit, trying to swallow it. When the next shot landed on his tongue, it triggered Tucker's gag reflex, forcing him to pop off Rigel's spurting erection.

Even as Tucker coughed and swallowed, he had just enough presence of mind to keep jacking Rigel's erection, working him through his release. A couple of his lover's ejaculates streaked across Tucker's face, and he heard Rigel groan his name once more. Leaning back to miss Rigel's last couple of shots, Tucker stared at the pleasure-pain expression twisting the man's expression.

Stunning.

When Rigel finished shooting, he grinned down at him. "Damn, but I love marking you."

As Rigel swiped his finger through a dollop of seed on his cheek and brought it to his lips, Tucker realized marking him had to be a part of the shifter's nature—marking what was his. The bite mark to his neck made sense. A niggle of jealousy washed through him, too.

"How many have you bitten, Rigel?" Tucker demanded, the words out of his mouth before he could stop himself. Lifting his hand, he touched near where Rigel had left his scar. "How many others wear your mark?"

"None but you," Rigel growled, his eyes narrowing. Reaching down, he grabbed Tucker underneath his arms and hauled him to his feet. Holding him close, Rigel pinned him with a feral gaze. "You are the only one who will ever wear my mating mark, Tucker. You are my mate. Only you."

Tucker realized the bite had to be damn significant for Rigel to react so possessively. "You save it for your one and only?"

Rigel nodded once, his eyes dark with renewed need. "Yes," he confirmed, sliding a hand up Tucker's arm to tease along his shoulder. "Only you will ever wear my external mark." Then his eyes narrowed, and a feral growl erupted from him. "And I will renew it while marking you internally for centuries to come."

Dismissing the centuries comment, Tucker focused on what he thought was important. "Mark me internally?" When Rigel gave one slow nod, Tucker asked, "You want to do me bareback?"

"It's the only way to complete our bond," Rigel told him. Without waiting, he lifted Tucker and tossed him over his shoulder, palming his ass as he began moving. "I will spill my seed deep inside you and sink my teeth in your neck again. I will bond us, twining our lives for all eternity."

The breath whooshed from Tucker's lungs, and he wouldn't have been able to answer even if he'd wanted to. A few seconds later, he was able to suck in a much-needed lungful of air when Rigel tossed him onto the mattress. His lover didn't follow him down.

Instead, Rigel prowled around the bed to the nightstand. He was naked once more, telling Tucker he must have stepped out of his sweats as he walked. Rigel opened the drawer and pulled out a tube of lube, tossing it onto the bed beside Tucker's shoulder.

"If you don't want this," Rigel stated, pausing even as he raked Tucker with a feral gaze. "I need to know now. I'll need to leave." He stroked his still-hard dick, his chest rising and falling in deep breaths. "Because once I get on that bed with you." Rigel met Tucker's gaze, pinning him with one of heated need. "I won't stop until we're one."

Even as Tucker appreciated the warning, the out, he knew he wouldn't take it. He wanted what Rigel was offering with every fiber of his being. Tucker would finally have someone of his own, someone that would care for him just as much as he wanted to care for Rigel.

"Tucker?"

Hearing Rigel's growling of his name, Tucker snapped his attention back to his shifter's face and the hungry expression there. "I want this," he assured. Grabbing the hem of his polo shirt, he yanked it over his head. "I want you." Tucker unbuttoned and unzipped his jeans and began working them down his hips. "Want us."

With a roar, Rigel leaped onto the bed.

Tucker's shoes, socks, jeans, and underwear were gone in seconds. Gripping Tucker's calves, Rigel urged him to spread them, which he did eagerly. He welcomed his lover between his thighs, cocking out his knees in invitation.

Rigel groaned as he grabbed the lube. "Don't want to hurt you," he hissed as he met Tucker's gaze. The hunger in his expression was tempered by worry as he squirted a dollop of slick onto his fingers. "I'm gonna suck you while opening you," Rigel told him. "Get you nice and relaxed."

"Yessss," Tucker hissed, reaching for Rigel. He was all on board for that. His cock throbbed and twitched, betraying exactly how he felt.

When Rigel buried his face in Tucker's pubes and inhaled noisily, licking around the base of his shaft, Tucker shuddered. "Rigel," he cried, jerking his hips, needing more.

Rigel didn't disappoint. He lifted his head, opened his mouth, and swallowed Tucker to the root. The hot wet suction of Rigel's mouth quickly went to Tucker's head. Coupled with the way his lover massaged his stomach, tweaked his nipples, and teased along the flesh of his sides, Tucker soon lost himself in sensation.

Tucker writhed on the comforter, reveling in the heady sensations coursing through his body. Shudders wracked him. His cock ached. Before Tucker even knew it, he found himself coming hard, pouring his release into Rigel's sucking mouth.

As Tucker floated on the clouds of endorphins from his release, he barely registered when Rigel released him. His big lover levered over him, and he wrapped his arms around him on instinct. A second later, Tucker felt Rigel's thick cock head prod his entrance. A fresh wave of need surged through him, and he canted his hips in invitation.

"That's it, my mate," Rigel whispered into his ear. "Push out and let me in."

In the next instant, Rigel thrust forward, sinking his erection deep into Tucker's body in one long slow glide. His hot flesh against his own inner walls pulled a gasp from Tucker. Without the latex barrier, everything felt amplified, setting his nerve endings on fire.

Groaning, Tucker clung to Rigel, needing him close, or he felt he would float away.

Rigel gripped Tucker's thigh and pulled it high on his hip, opening him further. The position allowed Rigel's length to push just a little bit deeper, and Tucker groaned with pleasure. He felt so full, so stretched, and his chute muscles sent tingles of delight up his spine.

Then Rigel began to rut, nailing Tucker's gland with each stroke.

Barking Rigel's name, Tucker dug his fingers into the shifter's thick shoulders and hung on for the ride. He did his best to cant his hips and rock into each roll of his lover's hips, but he soon lost the rhythm. The mouth at his neck was the last straw, and Tucker lost himself in sensation as his orgasm washed over him again.

When Rigel's teeth pierced his neck, Tucker felt as if his orgasm would never end. Black spots danced across his vision, and he moaned as he sailed away on wings of ecstasy.

Tucker wasn't certain how long he was out, but when he woke, he felt damn amazing. It took him a moment to realize that somehow, Rigel had rolled them. His lover lay on his back, and Tucker was sprawled over his chest.

Rigel was gently stroking up and down his back. He breathed deeply, and every once in a while, his lover pressed a kiss to the side of his head. When Tucker clenched his chute muscles, Rigel grunted, and he realized his lover still had a mostly hard cock in his ass.

Ooookay.

"Relax, my mate," Rigel urged, rubbing up and down his back once more. "It's normal. I promise." He bussed another kiss to Tucker's temple. "Shifters have a naturally high sex drive, and I've wanted you again for a week." Slowly rocking his hips, Rigel eased his erection deeper, then partway out again. "I'll soften after another release or two."

"Or two?" Tilting his head, Tucker peered at Rigel questioningly. "Wow."

Rigel took advantage and pecked a kiss to his lips. His smile appeared sated even though his dick was still hard. Sighing deeply, Rigel gazed at Tucker with what could only be called an adoring expression, the look making his dark eyes almost light up.

"Yeah, probably," Rigel murmured, but he didn't sound concerned. "After that, we'll clean up, eat, and then track down your sister. We have a lot to explain to her." His big lover teased down his spine, mumbling, "Maybe a nap in there somewhere."

Tucker felt Rigel flex his hips again, heard and felt his rumbly hum of pleasure beneath him, and enjoyed the delicious tingles shooting through his rectum. Relaxing his cheek onto Rigel's chest, he decided he would be more than happy to follow his shifter's plan. After so many years of hiding, Tucker realized he wouldn't have to do that anymore.

With the help of his shifter, Tucker would finally be free to live his life.

About the Author

Charlie started writing fantasy when she was eight, and after stumbling onto her first erotic romance at age nineteen, she realized her true calling. She now focuses on writing gay erotic romance, normally of the paranormal variety, with heroes of all kinds. With the help and support of her husband, Charlie finally fulfilled one of her life-long goals . . . move to acreage with her horses. You can often find her curled up with her laptop and a cup of tea or glass of wine, creating her next adventure. Charlie enjoys exploring the mountains of her new Oregon home on horseback, 4-wheeler, or motorcycle.

She can be reached at ch.richards2010@yahoo.com

Or visit her at www.charlie-richards.com.

www.ingramcontent.com/pod-product-compliance
Lightning Source LLC
Chambersburg PA
CBHW070455130626
46555CB00003B/1006